The Daring Escape of The Misfit Menagerie

The Daring Escape of The Misfit Menagerie

Jacqueline Resnick

Illustrated by Matthew Cook

razOr
bill

An Imprint of Penguin Group (USA) Inc.

The Daring Escape of the Misfit Menagerie

RAZORBILL

Published by the Penguin Group
Penguin Young Readers Group
345 Hudson Street, New York, New York 10014, U.S.A.
Penguin Group (USA) Inc., 375 Hudson Street, New York, New York 10014, U.S.A.
Penguin Group (Canada), 90 Eglinton Avenue East, Suite 700, Toronto, Ontario, Canada
M4P 2Y3 (a division of Pearson Penguin Canada Inc.)
Penguin Books Ltd, 80 Strand, London WC2R 0RL, England
Penguin Ireland, 25 St Stephen's Green, Dublin 2, Ireland (a division of Penguin Books Ltd)
Penguin Group (Australia), 250 Camberwell Road, Camberwell, Victoria 3124, Australia
(a division of Pearson Australia Group Pty Ltd)
Penguin Books India Pvt Ltd, 11 Community Centre, Panchsheel Park, New Delhi – 110 017,
India
Penguin Group (NZ), 67 Apollo Drive, Rosedale, Auckland 0632, New Zealand
(a division of Pearson New Zealand Ltd)
Penguin Books (South Africa) (Pty) Ltd, 24 Sturdee Avenue, Rosebank, Johannesburg 2196,
South Africa

Penguin Books Ltd, Registered Offices: 80 Strand, London WC2R 0RL, England

10 9 8 7 6 5 4 3 2 1

Copyright © 2012 Penguin Group (USA) Inc.

ISBN 978-1-59514-588-8

Library of Congress Cataloging-in-Publication Data is available

Printed in the United States of America

They say it takes a village to raise a child, but for me, it took a village to make a writer. I dedicate this book to my village: Fred, Susan, and Lauren Greenberg, and Nathan Resnick.

Mumford's "Misfit Menagerie"

Staff

Misfit Menagerie Melts Hearts!

At Mumford's Farm & Orchard, apples aren't the only treats for kids. A field of oak trees conceals a different kind of find altogether: a menagerie of animals that could melt the hardest of hearts. The menagerie belongs to Thaddeus Mumford, the farm's owner. "I didn't set about to collect a menagerie," Mumford stated. "It just sort of happened."

Take Tilda the Angora rabbit, for example. Mumford was about to buy dinner at a local fair when he noticed a commotion over by the carousel. A rabbit—so white and fluffy she could be mistaken for a cloud—was being raffled off. "Before I knew it, I was using my dinner money to buy a raffle ticket," Mumford explained. "That night I took Tilda home with me." Now Tilda, a favorite of little girls, spends her days hopping around Mumford's farm.

Mumford acquired his hairy-nosed wombat, aptly named Wombat, at the city train station. "I was planning to get a ticket to visit my brother," he told the *Daily Journal*, shaking his head. "But outside the station, a man was selling animals from a shut-down zoo." Mumford observed as the man sold animal after animal until the only one left was a small, brown creature that resembled a piglet. "I didn't even know what kind of animal it was," he recounted with a laugh. "But before I knew it, I was using my train money to bring him home." Now Wombat passes his days expertly burrowing his way through throngs of admirers at Mumford's farm.

Rigby, a one-year-old Komondor dog, was the first of the menagerie to be born on the farm. His mother was a lost dog who happened to wander onto Mumford's property. "I spent a whole day thinking I'd left a mop head in my yard," Mumford told the *Daily Journal*. "Finally I realized it was a dog!" Eventually he identified the dog's owner, but by that time, she had already given birth to a litter. "When the dog's owner offered me a puppy as a thank-you, I just couldn't refuse," Mumford said. Now Rigby—who like all Komondor dogs is covered entirely in long, white ropes of fur—delights children at Mumford's farm with his penchant for what the crowds have affectionately dubbed "playing mop."

Of the menagerie, there's one animal that is clearly the star attraction: the bear with the never-ending tongue. That's how kids refer to Smalls the sun bear. Sun bears are the smallest member of the bear family—around the same height as a ten-year-old boy—and are distinguished by a yellow marking on their chest in the shape of a horseshoe and a slender, pink tongue that stretches to over twice the length of a human one. Like many sun bears, Smalls was born in Asia, but at six months old he was shipped to America to be auctioned off. As luck would have it, Mumford was present at that auction.

"I was looking to buy some chickens for my farm," Mumford explained. "But then Smalls got up onstage." At that moment, a fly buzzed past and Mumford witnessed Smalls "light up like a kid on his birthday." Instantly, Smalls bounded after the fly. Just when it appeared that the fly might get away, Smalls extended his extraordinarily long tongue and used it to snatch the fly right out of the air. "Before I knew it, I was bidding on a sun bear," Mumford said.

Mumford may never have gotten his chickens, but he argues that he got something much more valuable. Thanks to the yellow horseshoe on Smalls's chest and his uncanny ability to find four-leaf clovers, Mumford has deemed him his "lucky charm." Today, kids clamor to watch that lucky bear at Mumford's farm bound up trees and perform endless tricks with his long, graceful tongue.

With each passing year, the fame of Mumford's menagerie continues to grow as people pass along news of this unique group of animals to friends and neighbors. The animals have even earned themselves a popular nickname: the Misfit Menagerie. If you're interested in giving Smalls, Rigby, Wombat, and Tilda a gander for yourself, just be warned: their crowd of fans becomes larger every day.

Chapter One
Battle of the Clover

Smalls the sun bear stood in the crook of his favorite oak tree, surveying the land below. It was a typical fall Saturday at Mumford's Farm & Orchard. Sprigs of orange and gold wove through the bushes, the smell of ripe apples dusted the air, and leaves fluttered to the ground like handfuls of confetti.

Over by the rosebushes, Tilda the Angora rabbit was at step three of her sixteen-step grooming process, picking apart strands of fur that had dared to clump together overnight. Next to the creek, Rigby the Komondor dog was admiring a fallen leaf between his paws, and under the shade of an oak tree, Wombat the hairy-nosed wombat was snoozing away in the hole he'd just finished burrowing.

Everyone was relaxed and idle, and Smalls didn't like it one bit. He knew exactly what came after idleness: boredom.

There will be no boredom on my *farm,* Smalls thought. Clearing his throat, he called out, "Attention!"

Down on the ground, Tilda continued on to step four of her daily grooming process, fastidiously straightening the red bow she wore on the top of her head. Meanwhile, Rigby moved on to another leaf, and Wombat let out a rumbling snore.

"Holy horseshoe," Smalls grunted, rubbing lightly at the yellow marking of a horseshoe on his chest. Silently, he began making a list. *How to Liven Things Up,* he called it. Smalls was a master list maker. Rarely a day passed by where he didn't make some sort of list. Lists of games he wanted to play, lists of Rigby's favorite colors, lists of ways to get Mumford to bring him more honey. No list was too short or too long for Smalls. He was, he liked to think, a list connoisseur.

How to Liven Things Up

1. Announce (loudly) that it's game time.

2. Introduce everyone to my newest, most exciting game yet.

3. PLAY!

Smalls nodded to himself. It was a good, solid plan, especially number three. In Smalls's opinion, playing could solve most anything. Rising onto his hind legs, Smalls pounded his thick black paws against the trunk of the oak tree. "Animals of Mumford's Farm & Orchard," he announced, his deep voice rolling through the farm. "I am pleased to tell you that it's officially game time!"

It worked. Rigby dropped his leaf. Tilda looked up from her grooming. And Wombat opened one eye, peering drowsily up at Smalls.

"Are we playing Mud Pile Dodge?" Tilda squeaked excitedly, fluffing out her fur.

"No, Speed Fetch," Rigby panted. "It's my . . . my . . ." He trailed off as a bird flew overhead. "Persimmon," he murmured, studying the bird's wings. "And magenta. Ooh, and a hint of aqua too!"

"This is a new game," Smalls told them. "I call it Battle of the Clover." He reached behind his ear, where he liked to tuck away the four-leaf clovers he was always stumbling upon. "I have in my paw a perfect four-leaf clover," he announced, holding it up for everyone to admire. Its green leaves glistened in the sun, still damp with morning dew. "Whichever team is the first to capture this clover and swim it to the end of the creek wins the game!" He bounded down to the ground, placing the clover on top of an old tree stump.

"I would like to formally request Tilda as my partner,"

Wombat jumped in, giving Tilda a loving tap with his snout.

Smalls nodded. "Then the teams are formed." He cleared his throat. "On your mark. Get set. Play!" Instantly, all four animals took off for the tree stump. Wombat, with his strong burrower's legs, got there first. But before he could grab the clover, Rigby took a flying leap forward, snatching it right up from under his snout.

"Bring it to me, Rigby!" Smalls called out. Holding the clover between his teeth, Rigby raced toward Smalls. But halfway there, an interesting cloud passed overhead.

Rigby looked up. "A squirrel," he whispered through his clenched teeth, studying the shape of the cloud. "No, a bone!"

Rigby was so focused on the cloud that he didn't notice the rock rising from the ground in front of him. "Watch out, Rigby!" Smalls shouted. Rigby let out a surprised bark as his eyes landed on the rock. At the very last second, he leapt up, narrowly avoiding it. But as he did, the clover slipped out of his teeth, flying wildly into the air.

Tilda broke into her fastest hop, her red bow flapping on her head. "I'm coming for you, clover!" she yelled. For a small rabbit, she could move surprisingly fast. But Smalls knew it didn't matter. Because he had a secret weapon.

Bounding next to her, he rose onto his hind legs and unfurled his long, slender tongue. As he used it to snatch the clover out of the air, several cheers erupted behind him. Smalls's fur bristled with excitement. Cheers could only mean one thing. The crowd had begun to arrive.

Chapter Two

Invisible Boy

The motorcar gave a sudden jerk, sending Bertrand Magnificence tumbling across the backseat. He clenched his teeth as he straightened back up. His uncle Claude rarely drove the motorcar himself, and now Bertie—as he preferred to be called—understood why. *He* could probably drive it better, and he was ten. He pressed his nose against the window, watching the farms tumble past outside, barns and corn fields and houses falling away like dominoes. He tried to remember what state they were in today, but he never could keep track. Pennsylvania? Massachusetts? North Carolina? He gave up. It didn't matter much anyway; in a few days, they'd be somewhere else.

Bertie pushed a strand of shaggy red hair out of his eyes. Ever since his uncle had shoved him into the backseat earlier, he'd been wondering where they were going. Of course, he did know where they *weren't* going—and that was to visit his mom. Sometimes, when they stopped in a new city or a new town, it would hit Bertie that this could be it: the place where she lived. But anytime he worked up the nerve to ask his uncle, Claude would just laugh or spit a chewed-up fingernail in his face. "Keep your mind on your job, boy," he'd sneer.

Bertie took a deep breath, squaring his shoulders. "Where are we going, Uncle?" he asked cautiously, careful to banish any speck of curiosity from his voice. Curious was the third-worst thing a boy could be, according to his uncle, firmly behind talkative and the worst crime of all, happy.

"I have an errand to run," Claude said vaguely, reaching up to stroke his long, white beard. "It's of no importance to you, boy, so keep quiet! You're just here to watch the motorcar while I attend to my business. You never know what vagrants and thieves are lurking around these parts."

Bertie leaned back in his seat, frustrated. In all the years he'd lived with Claude, Claude had never once taken him to the hospital where his mom was cared for. Bertie knew next to nothing about the hospital—only that Claude called it the loony bin. "After your dad died in the accident, your mom lost her marbles," he'd told Bertie once. "This loony bin was the only place that would take her." Bertie stifled a groan. He wished he could just grab the wheel and steer them straight to the hospital himself. But of course, he couldn't. Because he had no idea where it was. Like always, the thought left him feeling sour, as if he'd swallowed a whole lemon and it had gotten stuck somewhere between his throat and his heart.

The motorcar jerked again, sending Bertie flying headfirst into the front seat. "What is wrong with you, boy?" Claude seethed. He pushed Bertie away, one of his jagged fingernails catching on his cheek. Bertie cried out as the nail sliced his skin, drawing blood. "Get back to your seat!" Claude demanded.

As Bertie scrambled away from his uncle, he knocked a stray piece of paper to the floor. Quickly, he bent down to retrieve it. It was an article, torn out of a newspaper. *Misfit Menagerie,* he began to read, but before he could get any further, Claude reached back, snatching it out of his hands. "Stop reading," he snapped.

Bertie dug a nail into his palm, making tiny half-moons on its surface. "Yes, Uncle," he said dully.

"You know how I feel about children and *reading,*" Claude continued. He chewed on a fingernail, spitting it out on the ground. "Now, pretend you're invisible and let me drive in peace!"

Bertie dug another half-moon into his palm as he shrank

into the backseat. *Invisible Boy,* he thought. He liked that one. He'd be a hero who had the power to turn invisible with just the blink of an eye. Bertie was always dreaming up hero counterparts for himself. He liked to imagine that if he tore off his too-short pants and torn-up shirt and old suspenders, he'd become someone else altogether, someone who could stop time or lift houses or, best of all, sprout wings and fly away.

Being invisible could be very useful, he decided. He could sneak into Claude's room and drink up his entire urn of hot cocoa. He could eat huge meals—hot, succulent, delicious meals—and no one would be able to stop him. Maybe he could even find a way to befriend the new girl, Susan, without Claude punishing him. Bertie blinked once, twice, three times. But when he held his hand out in front of him, it was still there: five fingers, one freckle, completely visible.

With a sigh, he leaned against the window again. Outside, the farms were growing smaller, the trees taller. In the distance he saw a splash of red, pouring across the horizon. It was an apple orchard, he realized as the motorcar rattled closer. Maybe that meant he'd get a glass of apple cider out of this trip! The thought snuck up on him, and he almost burst out laughing at the absurdity of it. It wouldn't matter how inexpensive the cider was; Claude would never let him have it. *Little boys do not deserve luxuries like cider,* he imagined Claude saying in his nasal whine.

One day, Bertie promised himself. One day he'd get fresh cider from an orchard and ride a bike down a rolling hill and buy a triple-scoop cone from an ice cream stand. He was just picturing how he would dangle his feet in a swimming hole while eating the cone when Claude made a sudden sharp turn, sending Bertie's head banging into the window. Fuzziness exploded behind his eyes. Outside, the road branched off into a dozen different directions as they followed a sign for ORCHARD. Bertie rubbed at his eyes, trying to see where they all led to. But by the time the fog in his head had cleared, the intersection was gone.

Chapter Three
A Dandelion Puff

At Mumford's Farm & Orchard, the Battle of the Clover was still raging on. Smalls dodged Tilda. He darted around Wombat. With the clover balanced carefully on his tongue, he dove into the creek.

"Look at Smalls!" he heard a boy in the crowd exclaim.

"His tongue's so long, Dad," a girl chimed in.

"Swim like the wind, Smalls!" Rigby cheered. Of course to the human ear, it just sounded like a series of barks.

"Do you think Rigby is cheering on Smalls, Ma?" a boy asked.

"Probably not, honey," his mom replied gently. "Animals don't talk to each other like we do."

"We talk to each other quite well, thank you very much," Wombat snorted with an indignant toss of his snout.

As Smalls swam on in the creek, a black motorcar pulled

up behind Mumford's blue-shuttered house. The car was old and rickety, with splotches of peeled paint and a torn fabric roof that flapped open in the breeze. It let out a sputter of smoke as it creaked to a stop.

A man climbed out of the car. He was tall, with long, spindly legs and a huge belly that made him look like he might topple over at any second. His nose was far too big for his face, and the top of his head was completely bald. But the hair he did have—the patches on the side, his bushy eyebrows, his long beard—was all pure white. The man was dressed entirely in purple: shiny purple shoes, purple pants made of brushed velvet, a tight purple vest with purple buttons that looked ready to pop at any second, and a purple topcoat with coattails that swished behind him as he moved. In his hand he clutched a purple top hat with a silk purple ribbon along its brim.

The man placed the top hat on his head. In his other hand, he held an article torn out from a newspaper. He studied it as he crossed the farm's broad lawn, a scowl spreading across his face. "'Misfits' is right," he muttered to himself.

Back at the creek, the crowd was so focused on watching Smalls that no one noticed the strange man in purple edging closer. The man's scowl deepened as his eyes swept through the crowd. But then they landed on Smalls, and for the briefest of seconds, his lips twisted into a smile.

Smalls wasn't doing anything particularly special at the moment. But the fact of the matter was, Smalls *was* special. Tilda claimed his tongue was magnetic. Wombat liked to break out his French and say it was *je ne sais quoi*. But this man, with his angry scowl and purple top hat, whispered just one word—"money"—when he looked at Smalls.

The man pushed his way toward the creek. As Smalls climbed out of the water, the man moved even closer, stroking his white beard. He was so focused on Smalls that he almost didn't see the white ball of fur blocking his path. His eyes narrowed when he noticed Tilda. *"Animals,"* he muttered under his breath. "Always in the way." Lifting a shiny,

purple shoe, he gave Tilda a swift kick. Tilda let out a terrified squeal as she flew backward.

"The pretty rabbit!" cried a girl in a pink polka-dot dress.

"Oh my," the man said lightly. "I mistook her for a dandelion puff." He lifted his purple top hat, bowing slightly
to the girl and her mom. "My mistake." Smiling thinly, he
disappeared into the crowd.

Tilda scrambled to her feet, looking miffed. "A *dandelion puff*?" she exclaimed. "What *dandelion puff* has fur like
this?" She held out a paw. It was white as snow and smooth
as silk. "Wombat won't believe this."

Shaking off her fur, she hopped over to Wombat. But
he was in the middle of burrowing his way through a group
of kids, a wall of dirt spraying out behind him. Rigby too
was preoccupied, holding very still as a tiny wisp of a girl

hid beneath his mop-like fur and then—*pop!*—jumped up to surprise her parents.

Behind Tilda, a girl with blond pigtails was tossing kernels of popcorn to Smalls, who caught each one easily with his tongue. Smalls didn't notice as Tilda turned away with a grumpy "humph!" *Just one more and I'll break my own record,* he thought. He'd just stretched out his tongue to try again when a strange word caught his attention. It floated out from the huddle of parents chatting and gossiping while their children played: *menagerie.*

Smalls didn't know the meaning of the word, but it had a nice ring to it. He inched closer to the parents. "Look at this," one of the dads was saying. He held a bag of freshly picked apples in one hand and a newspaper in the other. "'Misfit Menagerie Melts Hearts,'" he read as he passed the newspaper along.

A woman in a red coat snatched up the paper. "'At Mumford's Farm & Orchard, apples aren't the only treats for kids,'" she read aloud. Smalls inched even closer. As the woman continued to read from the article, snippets drifted toward him. "Hardest of hearts . . . expertly burrowing . . . playing mop . . . bear with the never-ending tongue."

Smalls took a step back in surprise, barely noticing when a toothy boy tossed two popcorn kernels his way. "Holy horseshoe," he murmured. *They* were the menagerie.

Chapter Four

Honey, Honey, Honey

"All right then!" Thaddeus Mumford's voice rang out through the crowd. Mumford was the animals' owner, and "all right then" was his favorite phrase. He said it all the time. Sometimes it meant good morning, sometimes it meant good night, sometimes it meant good job. Right now it meant *show's over*. In Mumford's hands was a tray filled with the animals' evening meals. Smalls could smell the steam wafting off the bowl of warmed honey. He bounded quickly over to Mumford.

As the crowd dispersed, Mumford placed Smalls's bowl of honey next to his favorite oak tree. "You gathered quite the crowd tonight, my little lucky charm," Mumford said as he scratched Smalls under his chin. "My animals are becoming famous." He gave Smalls a final scratch before moving on to the others.

Immediately, the sweet smell of honey drew Smalls in. With a happy grunt, he stuck his muzzle into the bowl and let the warm honey coat his tongue. *Mmmm,* he thought as Mumford headed back to his house. *I do love honey.*

As the animals gobbled down their dinners, the sun began to set overhead, a night chill stealing through the air. Next to Smalls, Tilda let out an angry squeal as a drop of carrot soup landed on one of her paws. Wombat finished up his lemongrass stew and hurried over to her. "It's barely noticeable," he assured her. "You're still as resplendent as ever."

Tilda gave her fluffy white tail a proud twitch. "That means gorgeous," she informed Rigby.

Smalls tried not to laugh as he gave his bowl of honey a final lick. *Tilda crisis averted,* he thought. The honey had made him feel all warm and gooey inside, like a freshly baked cookie, and as he leaned back against his tree, his eyes drifted shut. He loved how, even at night, he could picture every inch of the farm. The field of dandelions that danced in the breeze. The tall oak trees that towered over everything. And of course, the stretch of apples in the distance, spilling across the horizon like red paint.

"It's Sunday tomorrow," he heard Tilda say to Wombat. "No crowds."

"I plan on reciting the entire French alphabet," Wombat replied. Wombat had spent a year in a Paris zoo and therefore considered himself an expert on the French language. "Forward *and* backward."

"Well, I plan on washing my bow in the creek so it's as resplendent as I am!" Tilda announced.

Wombat laughed. "That's a clever plan, my love." Sleep was slowly creeping into his voice, making it hang heavy in the air.

One by one, the animals drifted off to sleep. Meanwhile, miles away, the man in purple was lying in his own bed. Using his finger, he traced the shape of a horseshoe on top of his blanket. "Money," he said once more, a greedy smile creeping onto his face. Then, just like the animals, he too fell asleep.

Chapter Five

Bajumba

Sunday afternoon, Smalls was napping in his favorite oak tree when the sound of digging woke him. He looked down to see Wombat burrowing his way steadily through the dirt. "Careful, Wombat!" Tilda squealed as several grains of dirt landed on her otherwise immaculate paws.

But Wombat just kept on digging.

"Wombat?" Tilda tried again.

Still Wombat didn't respond.

"Wombat," Tilda repeated. "WOMBAT!"

Wombat's head snapped up. "Did you say something, Tilda?"

"Never mind." Tilda sighed. She eyed him anxiously. "Is everything okay? You're digging like a maniac."

Wombat sat back on his haunches. "I've been pondering my name," he explained. "You see, the problem with my name is that it's not, precisely, a name. It is more of a biological classification. A species, if you will. It would be like calling Rigby *dog*."

Smalls stood up in the tree, stretching out his paws. "What can you do about it?" he asked as he climbed down to the ground.

"I propose a name change," Wombat declared. "From here on in, I shall be referred to at all times as Fred."

"Fred?" Tilda squealed. "I'm now in love with a *Fred*?"

"Fred," Wombat confirmed. "I've always liked that name. It's a sturdy name, a solid name."

"Fred," Smalls tried out as he made his way to the creek. He was in the middle of a nice long drink when Rigby thrust a grass-stained paw in front of him.

"Hunter green," he exclaimed. Rigby loved to pretend his fur was other colors. "Who wants to be boring old *white*?" he was always saying.

"Looks nice—" Smalls began, but a strange sound cut him off. It came from Mumford's blue-shuttered house. Smalls looked over sharply, bending his ears forward. It was laughter, he realized. But it wasn't Mumford's. Mumford's laughter was like rain falling on the creek, soft and steady: *plop-plop, plop-plop, plop-plop*. This laughter wasn't soft, and it certainly wasn't steady; it was the laughter of a storm.

"What was *that*?" Tilda asked, hopping over to the creek. "It sounded . . ."

"Like laughter?" Wombat offered.

"Ominous!" Tilda finished. She looked proud of herself. *Ominous* was one of Wombat's favorite words.

Wombat laughed. "Dark clouds are ominous. A frozen stream is ominous." He patted Tilda with his snout. "Laughter is not ominous."

"Okay," Tilda agreed. After all, Wombat claimed to be nearly a genius. He swore he knew almost every word in the English language and often dreamed in French. "If you say so, Wombat."

"Fred," Wombat corrected, lifting his furry brown snout in the air.

Tilda coughed a little. "Right."

Smalls ignored them, keeping his eyes on the house. "Mumford is probably just having some friends over," he decided. He hadn't noticed anyone arrive, but there wasn't much that could rouse him from his Sunday afternoon nap.

Rising onto his hind legs, Smalls squinted in through the

kitchen window. The kitchen was empty, but he could just make out four shadows in the living room. The first—small and narrow—clearly belonged to Mumford. But he didn't recognize the other shadows: two wide and brawny and one tall and big-nosed, wearing what appeared to be a top hat. "Three friends," he determined, dropping back down.

Rigby's black nose twitched under his fur. "And a lot of elderberry cordial," he determined. The animals knew from experience that elderberry cordial was Mumford's drink of choice. Rigby looked like he was about to say something else when a strange word exploded from the house.

"BAJUMBA!"

"Bajumba?" Tilda echoed wonderingly. It was a word none of the animals had ever heard.

Smalls stared suspiciously at the blue-shuttered house. He knew all of Mumford's friends. There was Larry the Spitter, who could give you a shower with the letter S. There was Tall Thomas, who had to stoop whenever he was inside. And there was Smalls's favorite, Percival, who owned a candy store in town and snuck the animals gooey caramels whenever he visited. But Smalls didn't recognize this voice at all.

Inside, something shattered, making him jump. He pawed nervously at the ground. Something was off. He knew it in the same way he knew when rain was coming or a fog was rolling in: a feeling deep down in his bones. "Tilda's right," he said slowly.

"I am?" Tilda beamed.

Smalls nodded. "Something feels ominous." He paced along the creek, thinking. What if something was wrong? What if Mumford needed them? "We have to get inside," he decided. He turned to face the others. "We have to find out what's going on."

At once, Smalls, Wombat, and Tilda all looked at Rigby. He was the only one of them who could sneak unseen into the blue-shuttered house. He was just small enough to squeeze through the doggie door in the back, and once inside, it would be easy for him to blend in. Humans were always mistaking Rigby for a mop.

"Me?" Rigby croaked.

"You know you're the only one who can blend in, Rigby," Smalls replied gently.

Rigby sighed. "If I was hunter green, I wouldn't," he muttered. Shaking the fur out of his eyes, he took off for the house.

Chapter Six

It's Loyd, Not Lloyd

The inside of the blue-shuttered house usually smelled like raspberry sugar cookies. Mumford ate them by the bagful, their scent wafting after him like cologne. But today the smell of elderberry cordial overpowered everything, even the cookies. It was a sweet, sticky, pungent scent, the kind that tickled and taunted your nose.

Standing in the dim light of Mumford's mudroom, Rigby's nose twitched. It quivered. It trembled. It was about to sneeze. For some animals, a sneeze would be nothing, just a soft *achoo*. But when Rigby sneezed, whole houses shook. "Ah . . ." Rigby said. "Ah . . . AH . . ." He dove to the floor, burying his nose in his paws. "CHOO!" The sound was muffled by his thick mop of fur.

Rigby let out a shaky breath as he stood up again. He looked in the mirror hanging on the mudroom wall. "You're

a smooth, graceful dog," he told himself. "You're a smart, clever dog. You're a . . . very white dog." He took a step forward, examining himself in the mirror.

"A nice streak of violet could go right here," he murmured. "And a lovely streak of teal right here. And maybe some bright fuchsia over here—*stop*." He backed away from the mirror. "You have a job to do, Rigby," he told himself. Ducking his head, he crept into the living room, his footsteps muffled by the thick tufts of fur draped over his paws.

Mumford was seated at the table with three men, a deck of cards lying between them. Rigby dropped into his best mop-like pose, curling up in the corner with his face and paws tucked beneath his fur. Opening just one eye, he peeked out through several strands.

Two of the men seated at the table were identical twins. They had the same wide shoulders and the same brawny muscles and the same matching scowls. The third man, however, looked nothing like them. He was tall, with spindly legs and a round stomach and a nose that was far too large for his face. He was dressed from head to toe in red: shiny red shoes, red pants made of brushed velvet, a tight red vest with red buttons that looked ready to pop at any second, a red topcoat, and last but not least, a red top hat, with red feathers along its brim. The man gnawed on his thumbnail, then spit it out

on the ground. It landed a few inches from Rigby, just close enough for Rigby to see a tiny clump of cocoa powder stuck to the bottom of it.

In front of each man sat a glass of elderberry cordial. Mumford's was nearly empty. "Thithortchal ithivine," Mumford mumbled. He was trying to say, "This cordial is divine," but his words tumbled out too fast, running right into each other. Tipping his chair back, Mumford reached for his glass. But just as his fingers grazed it, he lost his balance. He rocked. He teetered. And then—*bam!*—he slid to the ground, landing with a thud.

Rigby stiffened in his hiding spot.

"Mumford, old boy!" the man in red exclaimed. He had a nasal voice, as if someone was pinching his oversized nose. "Are you okay?"

"Fine, Claude, fine," Mumford groaned.

With a wink at the twins, Claude quickly tipped some of his own cordial into Mumford's glass, filling it to the brim again.

Mumford mumbled something about a broken chair as he pulled himself up. For a second, he eyed his now-full glass, a crease forming between his eyebrows. "All right then," he said slowly, breaking into a smile. "Elderberry cordial, my favorite!" He picked up the glass, taking a big gulp.

"Oh yes," Claude simpered. "I know."

"We all know," one of the burly twins muttered under his breath. He whipped several cards out on the table.

"It's not your turn, Loyd," his twin scolded, tossing the cards back at him.

"Well, it's not *your* turn either, Lloyd," Loyd argued back.

"It's Mumford's turn, boys," Claude said smoothly. He narrowed his eyes at the twins and they both fell silent, sinking down in their chairs.

Mumford looked back and forth between the twins. They were even dressed the same, in identical, tight black shirts and matching fedoras. "You havtha samename?"

"Of course not!" Loyd said, looking offended.

"How silly!" Lloyd added, looking insulted.

Mumford blinked rapidly. "So you're Loyd." He pointed at the first twin. He looked at the second twin. "And you're . . . ?"

"Lloyd," the second twin said.

Mumford took another gulp of cordial, looking befuddled.

Claude cleared his throat. "It's simple, really," he explained in his nasal voice. "He's Loyd with one *L*." He pointed at the first twin. "Or maybe he's Loyd with one *L* . . ." he corrected, pointing at the second twin. He waved his hand through the air. "Well, *one* of them is Loyd with one *L* and the other one is Lloyd with two *L*'s. Now." He clapped his hands together. "I believe it's your turn again, Mumford."

"My turn?" Mumford mumbled, staring blankly at his cards.

Next to him, Claude drummed his fingers against the table. His fingernails were sharp and jagged, several bitten down to the quick. "That's right, old boy," he said cheerfully.

"Lessee . . ." Grabbing his glass, Mumford took another swig. A drop splashed onto Claude's shoe. "Whoopsie." Mumford chuckled.

Claude leapt up, his face reddening. "Why, you sloppy, dim-witted—"

Suddenly he fell silent, his eyes widening. Loyd and Lloyd jumped up behind him, their fists clenched. Mumford's eyes darted from the twins to Claude and back again. Claude quickly cleared his throat. "Ha ha," he sang out. "Just a little joke, of course." His voice was suddenly as sweet and sugary as cotton candy. He gestured for Loyd and Lloyd to sit down, and they both dove back into their chairs.

A vein bulged on Claude's neck, but he kept his voice cheerful. "A little spill never hurt anyone!" He walked over to Rigby, stopping only inches away from him. Rigby held his breath, lying stock-still. "Besides," Claude continued, wiping his shoe on Rigby. "It's on your mop now!"

He gave his shoe a final shine on Rigby's fur before returning to the table. "Now, where were we? Oh, right. Come on now, Mumford. Clock's ticking."

Mumford rubbed his bleary eyes. He ran a hand through his messy hair. Finally, he pulled out several cards, throwing them onto the table.

For a split second, Claude looked worried. Then, ever so slowly, he nodded. "Bajumba," he whispered. His fingers flew nimbly across the table as he spread out his cards. When he looked up, his brown eyes were glowing. "Don't forget what we agreed on, Mumford," he said. "This game is for everything."

Meanwhile, Rigby peeked through his fur, looking up at the window behind the table. His gaze grew distant as he watched a golden leaf float gently to the ground outside. Slowly, his eyes drifted shut. His breathing deepened. His paw twitched. And right there, in the middle of Mumford's living room, he dozed off.

Chapter Seven

A Bush, a Tree,
and a Pile of Dirt

The longer Rigby was gone, the more lists Smalls made. He'd already made a list of all the times Tilda had called herself beautiful in the last week (sixty-three), all the four-syllable words Wombat had used (thirty-nine), and his favorite foods other than honey (zero). Now he'd moved on to

Reasons Why Rigby Is Taking So Long

1. He found Mumford's stash of jasmine roasts.

2. He can't tear himself away from Mumford's painting of the apple orchard.

3. He is trying to determine if Mumford's chairs are more silver or gray.

4. He's fallen asleep.

Smalls laughed to himself. Who could fall asleep on a *spy* mission? He mentally scratched that off his list, replacing it with:

4. Mumford is blocking the exit.

Over by the tree stump, Tilda was frantically running through her sixteen-step grooming process, which she always did when she was nervous. "Step twelve," she muttered to herself. "Shine tail." She rubbed up against Wombat, giving her tail a nice buffing. "Step thirteen, sharpen nails." Lifting a paw, she filed her nails against a tree stump.

Smalls paced to the creek and back. That word—*bajumba!*—had left his nerves feeling all frayed. What did it mean? And who had said it? And why *had* Rigby been in there for so long? He couldn't take it any longer. "I think we should investigate," he said.

Tilda stopped mid–nose glossing, her ears perking up. "Like a spy game?"

"Yes!" Smalls nodded fervently. "What do you think, Wombat?"

Wombat peered irritably at Smalls. "The name is Fred," he said.

"Of course," Smalls said quickly. "What do you think, Secret Agent Fred?"

Wombat cocked his head. "Well, we'd have to be extremely clandestine. *And,*" he added, "it would be beneficial to camouflage." He scooped up a handful of dirt, smearing it over his paws. Then, using his teeth, he plucked several leaves off a nearby bush and held them out for Tilda.

"You want me to cover my fur in *that*?" she gasped.

"Wombat's right," Smalls said. Wombat shot him a look. "*Fred's* right," he corrected. "The more we blend in, the better."

Wombat carefully wove several leaves through Tilda's fur. "*Une belle lapin,*" he declared. "A beautiful bunny." Tilda brightened slightly. "Well," she said. "It *is* a little like dressing up . . . "

By the time the animals took off to investigate, they were completely camouflaged. Tilda was so covered in leaves that she looked more like a bush than a rabbit. Smalls had fashioned himself after a short tree. And Wombat was slathered head to toe in dirt.

"Look," Tilda breathed as they rounded the yard. Behind the house sat an old black motorcar. It was dirty and a little lopsided, with peeling paint and a black fabric roof that had a tear down the side.

"Mumford doesn't have a motorcar," Smalls whispered. He sniffed at the air. There was an odor wafting from the car, a mix of old dirt and moldy straw and something else, something he couldn't place. Quietly, Smalls crept closer until he was peering in through the car's window. The front seats were empty, but something caught his eye in the backseat. It was a boy.

The boy was fast asleep, huddled beneath a threadbare blanket. He had red hair that stuck out in wisps from beneath a baseball cap and dozens of tiny freckles the color of chocolate. A scratch ran down his cheek, a thin line of blood clotted over it.

Smalls inched toward the back window, wanting to get a better look. He had just pressed his nose against the glass when—*CRACK!*—a twig snapped in half beneath his feet. He froze in place, his heart leaping into his throat. Inside the car, the boy tossed under his blanket. Smalls held his breath, not moving a single muscle. But still the boy shifted. He yawned. He opened his eyes.

Chapter Eight

A Deal's a Deal

Inside the car, Bertie blinked several times. When his eyes landed on Smalls, they widened in surprise. *There's a bear at my window,* Bertie thought. The bear was small (for a bear) and coal black except for a yellow marking in the shape of a horseshoe on his chest. A cluster of leaves poked out from the fur on the top of his head. This wasn't just any bear, Bertie realized with a start. This was *the* bear.

That morning, Bertie had noticed a newspaper article sitting in the trash can. Before anyone could see him, he'd snatched it out, stuffing it under his shirt. Then he'd hurried into his room to read it. *Misfit Menagerie Melts Hearts!* the headline said.

Immediately, Bertie had been drawn into the article. His uncle didn't allow him to have books—"They fill boys' heads with rubbish," he claimed—but as Bertie read about the four unusual animals of Mumford's Farm & Orchard, he felt that warm rush of excitement that comes from a great story. And now, as he looked out at the bear pressed up against his window, Bertie was positive. This was him. Smalls, the bear with the never-ending tongue.

Slowly, Bertie placed his hand against the glass. "Hi," he whispered, looking into Smalls's dark brown eyes.

As the boy's bright blue eyes met his, Smalls thought of a hundred things at once: pillows made of leaves, the creek rippling softly over his paws, the way he used to curl up next to Mumford's hearth when he was a cub, letting the fire warm him deep in his bones.

Inside the car, Bertie moved closer to the window. "I'm Bertie," he said, even though he knew the bear couldn't understand him. He was about to say something else when he noticed a movement over by the blue-shuttered house. The back door of the house flung open and out stepped Loyd. Or maybe it was Lloyd. Bertie never could tell them apart. But he *could* read their expressions, and right now Loyd (or Lloyd) looked unusually happy.

Bertie gestured frantically for Smalls to run. If one of the Lloyds were coming, then his uncle could be close behind— and the last thing any bear needed was a visit from Claude Magnificence. "Hurry," Bertie whispered, trying to shoo him away. For a second Smalls just looked at him, something softening in his eyes. Then he turned and he ran. Two other animals followed behind him: a fluffy rabbit covered in leaves and what looked like a very dirty little piglet. They slipped out of sight just as Lloyd (or was it Loyd?) reached the car.

He opened the door, pushing Bertie roughly aside. "Forgot this," he grunted, grabbing a silver pen from the backseat. "And," he added with a dopey grin, "it looks like we're going to need it." Slamming the door shut, he stomped back to the house, leaving the motorcar quivering in his wake.

Inside the house, Rigby was slumbering away peacefully. Until suddenly: "Bajumba!"

Rigby bolted awake at the sound of the yell. Claude had leapt out of his chair and was now dancing around the living room. Lloyd and Loyd jumped up after him. "I won!" Claude shouted, tossing his top hat into the air.

The top hat landed on the table, right in front of Mumford. Wrenching his chair back, Mumford stood up. "You—you can't . . ." he stammered. "You can't really mean to . . ."

"Oh, but I can." Claude reached up to stroke his white beard. "And I do."

Behind him, Loyd and Lloyd guffawed gleefully, but when Claude glared at them, they both snapped their mouths shut in unison. "You know the rules of the game, Mumford,"

Claude said. "A deal's a deal." He paused next to a velvet-covered basket. Bending down, he wrested out a scroll of paper. As Lloyd, Loyd, and Mumford all gazed at the scroll, Rigby took it as his chance. With Claude's laughter ringing out behind him, he squeezed through the doggie door, slipping back into the world outside.

Chapter Nine

A Game for Everything

"*Finally!*" Tilda squealed as Rigby came trotting toward them. She looked out at him through a mask of green leaves. "What happened to you, Rigby?"

"I should ask you the same thing," Rigby replied, staring in disbelief at Tilda's leaf-covered coat. Smalls and Wombat had already jumped into the creek to wash off, but Tilda, who hated getting wet almost as much as she hated mud, had refused. She'd spent the past few minutes using her teeth to pick out each leaf one by one. So far she'd made it through two paws. "I haven't seen you this dirty since the lawn mower incident."

"It's not dirt," Tilda sniffed. "I'm in camo-flotch." As Wombat mouthed "camou*flage*" to Rigby, she picked another leaf out of her fur, spitting it onto the ground.

"What happened in there, Rigby?" Smalls asked anxiously.

He'd just started on a new list when Rigby came trotting back from the house. He called it *Who Are Mumford's Guests?* So far he'd come up with three possibilities.

1. *Professional card game players teaching Mumford a highly classified new game.*
2. *Apple pie bakers searching for the juiciest red apples in the land.*
3. *Salesmen of children, here to pawn off their latest shipment of little boy.*

Smalls knew that number three was highly unlikely, but he couldn't help but cling to the tiniest hope that Mumford's guests would be leaving the boy from the car behind. It would be nice, he thought, to have a boy living on the farm. Bertie, the boy had said his name was. Smalls fiddled with one of the four-leaf clovers behind his ear. He could invent so many new games to play with a Bertie.

"Well," Rigby began, but before he could continue, a door slammed in the back of the blue-shuttered house. Smalls signaled for silence as he strained his ears toward the sound.

On the other side of the house, Claude, Lloyd, and Loyd sauntered toward the rickety black motorcar. "Now *that* is how you play a game of cards," Claude said in his nasal voice. His red top hat was back on his head, and he reached up, carefully adjusting it. "Don't you agree, Loyd?"

"Absolutely," Lloyd said at the same time Loyd exclaimed, "Definitely!"

Lloyd glared at Loyd. "He was talking to me, Loyd."

Loyd elbowed Lloyd. "He was talking to *me*, Lloyd."

As they reached the black motorcar, both twins eyed the empty passenger seat. At the same time, they sprinted forward, elbowing and scratching and kicking each other to get to it.

"Mine!" Loyd gasped, hurtling forward.

"Mine!" Lloyd yelled, leaping in next to his twin.

They landed in a tangle of arms and legs, Lloyd sitting on top of Loyd, who was sitting on top of his fallen fedora. "Lloyd!" Claude scolded. "Get in the back!"

"He means you," Loyd said, his voice muffled from underneath his brother.

"No, he means *you*," Lloyd said, his scrunched-up knees knocking into his teeth.

"You!" Claude sounded exasperated. He grabbed Lloyd's arm. "Whichever one you are, get in the back NOW!"

Lloyd blew out a frustrated breath. He climbed into the backseat as the motorcar let out a sputter and a gasp, slowly kicking to life.

In the front of the house, Smalls caught a glimpse of the motorcar as it sped off down the road. For a second, right before a cloud of dust rose behind it, he saw a small, freck-led face peering out the back window. *So they didn't leave Bertie,* he thought, feeling a pang of disappointment. He looked over at Rigby, who was watching, mesmerized, as the dust settled back on the road. "What *did* happen in there, Rigby?" Smalls asked.

"They were drinking cordial and playing cards," Rigby said. "The game was For Everything. I've never heard of a card game called 'For Everything,' but that's what Claude said."

"Who's Claude?" Wombat asked.

"He's the boss. He was dressed completely in crimson. The color of blood," Rigby said with a shudder. "I don't know why he wouldn't choose a nicer shade of red. Like raspberry! Or ruby." He held up a paw, examining it. "A nice streak of ruby right here . . ." he murmured to himself.

As Rigby continued to ponder shades of red, Smalls paced up and down the length of the creek. "A game called For Everything," he mused out loud. Smalls loved games; he knew almost every card game Mumford played. But he'd never heard of a game called For Everything. Maybe number one on his list was right. Maybe they really *were* professional card players and For Everything was a highly classified new game. Or . . .

Suddenly, a thought occurred to Smalls. What if that wasn't the *name* of the game? What if, instead, it was what they'd been betting? Smalls had seen Mumford bet on card games before with Percival. Usually they played for caramels or malted milk balls. But what if this crimson Claude wanted to play *for everything*?

It made Smalls wonder: what, exactly, was *everything*?

"What else did you see, Rigby?" he asked.

"There was some kind of dance party," Rigby said thoughtfully. "It was very lively. The guests all danced around the living room."

"A dance party?" Smalls grunted, confused. What did a dance party have to do with a card game? "Anything else?"

Rigby thought for a minute. "There was a silver pen. And a scroll of paper."

"That's it?" Smalls crouched in front of Rigby. "Think hard, Rigby. Are you sure that's all you saw?"

Rigby shifted in place. He looked down at the ground, letting his fur flop into his eyes. "Yes," he said carefully. "That is all I *saw*."

Smalls paced faster along the creek. None of it made sense. Stopping next to the house, he rose onto his hind legs and peered in through the window. The downstairs was empty, no more shadows darkening the living room. All Smalls could see on the table was the faint outline of an empty glass and a small slip of paper.

He dropped back down. Mumford must have gone upstairs. On Sundays, when there were no crowds, Mumford liked to change into his pajamas before making the animals their evening meals. Smalls relaxed his jaw, which he hadn't realized he'd been clenching.

The game, whatever it was, was over, and Mumford was upstairs changing. It didn't matter what *everything* was; things were back to the way they should be. Soon, Mumford would come out with the animals' meals, the cuffs of his flannel bottoms trailing behind him. Feeling better, Smalls turned from the window.

As he did, a gust of wind blew open the back door of the house. It swept inside, rattling the empty glass and sending the slip of paper floating through the air. The paper landed faceup on the floor. Scrawled across it, in Mumford's sloppy handwriting, was some kind of list. The list was illegible, but the four red letters stamped on top of it were not. Separately, those four letters were harmless. They could mean anything. But when strung together, in just the right order, they built a very powerful word.

SOLD.

Of course, Smalls knew nothing of this word as he made

his way to his favorite oak tree. His mind was crowded with other words: *boy* and *warm* and *honey*. Sinking his claws into the tree's trunk, he began to climb. But when he was only halfway up, the fur on his paws suddenly stood on end.

A loud rumbling noise was coming from inside the blue-shuttered house. Snoring.

Smalls looked at Tilda. Tilda looked at Wombat. Wombat looked at Rigby.

Mumford had fallen asleep without preparing their evening meals.

In all the years the animals had lived with him, Mumford had never once forgotten their bedtime ritual. He always made sure that Smalls's bowl of warmed honey didn't drip into Wombat's lemongrass stew and that none of Tilda's carrot soup got on Rigby's jasmine roast. Smalls felt a cold shiver run down his back.

Something was ominous indeed.

No sooner had the thought entered his head than a second sound rang out through the air. It was a loud clanging coming down the street. As it drew closer, it blended with Mumford's snoring until an eerie melody echoed through the farm.

Snore-CLANG!-Snore-CLANG! Snore-CLANG!

"What, pray tell, is that cacophony?" Wombat asked.

Smalls didn't bother with a response; it would have been drowned out. Because suddenly, the cacophony was louder than ever. And it was coming from right behind them.

Chapter Ten

A Gilded Caravan

CLANG! CLANG! CLANG! The noise drew closer, drowning out Mumford's snores. *CLANG! CLANG! CLANG!* Smalls was just about to hide his ears under his paws when the source of the noise came into view.

It was the old black motorcar that had been parked in Mumford's driveway only minutes before. But now, hooked onto the back of it, was a caravan. Once upon a time, the caravan must have been a splendid affair: a deep red the color of rosebuds, with gilded curlicues that looped up and down and forward and backward, so every inch gleamed like a chest of gold. The caravan even had golden wheels that once must have glittered like sunlight as they spun.

But now, the caravan was old and grimy. Its red paint was faded and worn, its gilded spirals were dirty and chipped, and its golden wheels were caked in a layer of rust and dirt.

Something must have once been emblazoned above its single, barred window, but now only a few of the golden letters were left. *T e ost M g i ce r v li g C r*

Two doors in the black motorcar swung open, and Lloyd and Loyd climbed out. Slung over each of their shoulders was a strange-looking contraption. "That's them," Rigby whispered excitedly. "The men from the card game." Behind them, Claude leaned out the window, his crimson top hat sitting firmly on his head.

"That's Claude," Rigby said at the same time Tilda cried, "That's the man who kicked me!"

"He *kicked* you?" Wombat growled. "*Mon bel amour?*" He lifted a brown, furry leg in the air, which, although short, was rippling with muscles. "Don't fret, Tilda. I'll protect your honor with my own kick of retribution!"

"Wait." Smalls signaled for them to be quiet. Claude was saying something.

"Time for some action, boys," Claude said, rubbing his hands together eagerly. "I want one of you to take the rabbit and the dog and one of you to take the bear and that rat thing."

"Rat thing?" Wombat bristled.

"I choose the rabbit and the dog," Lloyd said immediately.

Loyd crossed his arms against his chest. "Why should I get stuck with the *bear*?"

"Because I said so?" Lloyd offered.

"Well, I said no," Loyd retorted.

"Yes."

"No."

"Yes."

"Lloyds!" Claude interrupted. "Is there a problem?"

"No, Boss," Lloyd said quickly. "Loyd was just saying that he would take the bear."

"Then get to it," Claude snapped.

Grumbling under his breath, Loyd stomped over to Smalls. "All right, you blimey bear. Make this easy for me and get in the caravan."

Smalls took a step back, eying the man warily. The man's muscles were bulging out of his black shirt, and his fedora sat crookedly on his head. Instantly, Smalls disliked his smell. He didn't smell like raspberry sugar cookies like Mumford or lavender essence like Tall Thomas or even broccoli stew like Larry the Spitter. He smelled rotten, like something inside him had gone bad.

"Get in the caravan!" Loyd ordered again.

Fear gurgled in Smalls's stomach. "Get in the caravan?" he repeated. "Why would I want to do *that*?"

Of course, all Loyd heard was a long series of bear grunts. "Don't mess with me, bear," he warned.

Out of the corners of his eyes, Smalls saw Lloyd scoop up Tilda. She wriggled desperately, trying to bite him, but Lloyd just laughed, easily snapping her mouth shut. A growl escaped from Smalls's throat.

"Fine." Loyd glared at Smalls. "You're not going to get in yourself? Then we'll do this the hard way!" Pulling the strange contraption off his shoulder, he snapped it over Smalls's face. Suddenly, Smalls's mouth was clamped shut. He couldn't move his tongue. He couldn't snap his jaw. Something hard was pressing against his nose. He was locked in a muzzle.

Smalls shook his head wildly. Who *was* this man? And where was Mumford? He tried making a list in his head to keep calm—the top ten games he'd ever invented—but it didn't help. Another growl escaped him, echoing off the oak trees.

"Don't try anything funny, bear." Loyd grabbed his muzzle, yanking him toward the caravan.

Over by the hammock, Lloyd clamped a similar muzzle onto Rigby. Rigby reared wildly, but Lloyd just jerked him down with a laugh. Rigby's eyes met Smalls's. There was a frantic look in them. *Do something,* they seemed to beg.

Smalls clawed angrily at his muzzle. Who did these men think they were, coming onto *his* farm and hurting *his* friends? He reared into the air, his claws glinting like knives. As far as bears went, Smalls was small. But as far as animals went, Smalls was big. He was strong. And he had claws that could slice straight through wood.

"I *said* not to try anything, you stupid bear," Loyd snarled. He gave the muzzle another yank and Smalls swiped at him automatically. Instantly, Smalls recoiled. He'd never, ever taken aim at a human before.

Loyd's face turned bright red as he sidestepped Smalls's claws. "I warned you, bear." He pulled something out of his pocket. It was long and thin and sharp. Smalls's eyes widened as he realized what it was.

A syringe.

Inside Smalls, something snapped. Suddenly, he wasn't Smalls anymore. He wasn't even a bear. He was anger, pure and red and fiery. Grabbing Loyd with one paw, Smalls drew the other one back, taking aim. Loyd writhed in his grip, but Smalls held on tight. He had him this time. One swipe and he'd be free.

With all the force he had inside him, years of bear instincts long buried and hidden, Smalls sliced through the air with his sharp claws. His paw was inches from Loyd's neck when something in the caravan caught his eye. A small, freckled face, peering out at him through the window.

Bertie.

Smalls looked into Bertie's bright blue eyes. Whatever had snapped inside him slowly clicked back together. The fiery anger was gone. He was Smalls again. He paused, and in that brief second, Loyd broke loose from his grip. He thrust the syringe into Smalls's shoulder, making Smalls cry out in surprise.

Smalls staggered backward. Immediately, he could feel the liquid from the syringe winding its way through him, making him feel warm and sluggish. The oak trees blurred before his eyes. "Much better," he heard Loyd say.

Smalls tried to pull away, but his paws felt heavy and numb, like they weren't his own anymore. Somewhere in the distance, he could swear he smelled honey, but when he tried to look for it, he found he couldn't move his head.

As Loyd dragged him toward the caravan, it was all Smalls could do to stay on his feet. The world spun and dipped around him, blackness slowly creeping in, draping everything in shadows. "Get in," Loyd snarled. "Boss is waiting for you. Though who knows why he wanted to win a lot of misfits like you."

As Smalls tumbled into the rickety, old caravan, he finally

understood. The card game they'd been playing . . . they *had* been betting for everything. And at Mumford's Farm & Orchard, the animals were everything.

Mumford had lost them.

It was the last thought Smalls had before the blackness swallowed him up.

Chapter Eleven

No Clouds Here

When Smalls opened his eyes, his first thought was that the world was melting. Silver dripped into blue that spiraled into red, colors spinning around him like a tornado. He blinked several times. Slowly, shapes began to emerge from the colors. A rough blue floor, chipped red walls . . . and silver bars. Only inches from his nose.

Smalls's heart tightened in his chest. Bars? Why were there bars?

Frantically, he reared up. The world tilted around him, but he managed to push himself to his paws—*ow!* The wall came out of nowhere, cracking into his head. He lost his balance, staggering backward into another wall.

Smalls's heart squeezed tighter. He grabbed the silver bars, pulling at them with all his might. But they wouldn't budge. And as the last of the fuzziness cleared from his eyes, he saw why. Clamped onto them was a huge black padlock. Smalls swayed on his feet.

He was locked inside a cage.

Breathing fast, he stuck his nose through the bars, peering out. Across from him sat a line of empty cages. They were all different sizes, from tiny to large. Streaked across the back of the largest cage was a red stain, a terrible odor wafting off it.

"This floor is sullying my fur!" Tilda's familiar whine was like music to Smalls's ears.

"Nice word choice, my love," Wombat said, sounding pleased.

Rigby let out a frustrated bark. "Who cares about *word choice*? I want to know where this thing is taking us!"

"I do as well," Wombat said softly. His voice broke, and he coughed quickly to cover it up.

"Are you worried now, Wombat?" Tilda asked. "Because you said you weren't worried, so I wasn't worried, but now if you're worried, then I should probably be worri—"

"I'm not worried, Tilda," Wombat cut in soothingly. "I'm . . . undaunted. I'm cavalier. I'm *très calme*!"

Smalls cleared his throat. "Wombat?" he asked shakily. "Tilda? Rigby?"

"Smalls!" Relief flooded Tilda's voice. "You're awake!"

"Where are you?" he asked. He rocked back on his heels, feeling dizzy. He wasn't used to having his vision blocked by walls. At Mumford's everything was wide and open, grass below him and orchards beside him and sky above him.

"I'm in the cage adjacent to yours," Wombat said.

"That means *next to*," Tilda piped up. "And I'm in the cage above his."

"And then there's me, beneath both of them," Rigby finished.

"What . . . happened?" Smalls asked. He felt like his memories had been spun into a web, all tangled together and stretched thin as thread.

"After examining the evidence," Wombat said, "I would venture to guess that we've been taken."

"We've been in this caravan forever." Rigby sighed. Smalls could hear him swishing his tail across the floor of his cage. "And I can't see a single cloud through this roof!"

"At least they took those ugly muzzles off you and Smalls," Tilda said helpfully. "They really weren't your best look."

Muzzles.

Suddenly, the cobweb in Smalls's mind splintered, a thousand different threads breaking loose. The muzzles. The men. The syringe. And the discovery.

Mumford lost us, Smalls remembered. He felt like someone

had kicked him in the gut. How could Mumford do that to them? To *him*? Mumford had brought him home when he was just a cub. He'd called him his lucky charm because of the four-leaf clovers he was always finding, and he brought him into the house on rainy nights. When Mumford caught pneumonia, Smalls spent five straight days curled up at the bottom of his bed, making sure his toes never got cold. Other than a few faint memories of a jungle in Asia, Mumford was all Smalls had ever known.

Smalls reached up nervously to touch the four-leaf clovers behind his ear. But he felt only fur. His clovers were gone. He swallowed hard. For the first time in many years, he felt anything but lucky.

Suddenly, the caravan took a sharp turn, sending the animals tumbling through their cages. Smalls rammed into a wall, pain erupting in his shoulder where the syringe had stabbed him. "Not my fur!" Tilda yelped as her paw caught on a loose nail, wrenching out several strands of fur. Gingerly, Smalls righted himself, gritting his teeth to keep from yelling out in pain.

"I do have one question," Wombat said. "Where, precisely, was Mumford during all of this?"

Smalls looked down at the rough, cracked floor of his cage. There was a brown strand of fur wedged into one of the crevices. It made him wonder who had been there before him.

"I guess he was sleeping," Tilda said, but she didn't sound very convinced.

Smalls sagged against the wall. He had the strangest feeling in the back of his throat, like one of Tilda's hair balls had gotten wedged back there. He couldn't bear the thought of telling the others what he knew. Why should they have to suffer too?

"Yes," he said, his deep voice resounding through the caravan. He couldn't believe how calm he sounded when inside it felt like every single one of his bones was rattling. "Mumford was just asleep, that's all. He must not have heard a thing." It wasn't a lie exactly, but it wasn't the truth either, and the words felt strangely rough on his tongue, like a piece of dry tree bark.

Rigby stuck his nose through the bars of his cage, his long tufts of fur obscuring his eyes. "But he'll come for us, right?" he asked softly.

I really hope so, Smalls thought. But out loud he said, "I'm sure everything will be fine, Rigby."

The words had just left his lips when the brakes let out a shriek. Slowly, the caravan skidded to a stop. Wherever they were going, they had arrived.

Chapter Twelve

A Lord in Chains

Smalls heard the Lloyds before he saw them. "My foot-steps are definitely louder than yours," Loyd said.

"You must have wax in your ears," Lloyd replied. "Because my footsteps are definitely louder than yours."

They clomped into the caravan, each trying to out-stomp the other. "No damage over here!" Loyd announced.

"What?" Lloyd yelled back. "I can't hear you over all this stomping!" Glaring at each other, they both gave a final stomp before falling still.

"I *said* no damage over here." Loyd was peering into Tilda's cage. "The rabbit didn't even try to gnaw through the wood."

"Wood?" Tilda tossed her fur indignantly. "I'm a long-haired, snow-white Angora rabbit, not a woodchuck!"

Loyd grimaced. "That rabbit's squeak is giving me a headache." He moved on to Smalls's cage, wrapping his thick hands around the bars. Smalls growled softly, remembering how they'd plunged the syringe deep into his shoulder. "No damage in here either," he announced.

"Except to the bear," Lloyd added, coming up behind him.

Both twins burst out laughing. "Good one, Lloyd," Loyd said.

"And Mom said we were too dumb to be funny." Lloyd shook his fist at the ceiling. "Who's the dumb one now, Mom?" Still chuckling, they both headed out of the caravan.

"Where are they going?" Tilda asked anxiously. "They can't just leave us here!"

"Of course not," Wombat consoled her. He looked up at the wall that separated him from Tilda. On the other side, Tilda did the same. "They'll come back for us, *mon lapin*," he promised.

With her head leaning against the wall, Tilda closed her eyes. "If you say so, Fred."

But as the seconds melted into minutes and the minutes turned into an hour, Smalls began to wonder. There was a small, barred window on the side of the caravan, but it was too small and too high to be of any use to them. Smalls had never felt so helpless in his life. Tapping his paw against the bars of the cage, he began to make a list.

Exciting Places We Could Be

1. A bee colony where honey is made.

2. A honey factory where honey is jarred.

3. A honey store that sells all kinds of honey.

He was hard at work on number four when a familiar smell wafted into the caravan. Smalls scrambled to the front of his cage. Peanuts. It smelled like peanuts. His stomach yawned inside of him, emptier than his honey bowl after he'd licked it clean. "Do you smell that?" he asked the others.

Smalls could hear Rigby sniffing wildly at the air. "It's coming closer," he said. "Closer. Clos—"

The door to the caravan swung open. "Don't you dare try any shenanigans on us, you monster," Loyd said. He and Lloyd stomped back inside. They each held one end of a thick rope in their hands.

Lloyd gave the rope an angry yank. "Get in here," he said.

"Now!" Loyd added with a yank of his own.

Into the caravan walked an enormous elephant, the ground trembling with each step he took. He was the gray of the sky after it rained, with ears as wide as wings and a trunk that swept the ground. His skin was thick and leathery, and on either side of his trunk were short, ivory stubs where his tusks once were. The elephant lifted his trunk, and Smalls noticed a streak of peanut butter along its tip.

The peanut butter on his trunk, Smalls realized. That's what he'd been smelling. He sank onto the floor, his stomach growling. In his mind he could picture a bowl of warmed honey sitting next to his oak tree. It was so vivid, he wanted to reach out and touch it, scoop the warm, gooey goodness up in his paws.

Lloyd and Loyd gave the rope another tug. It was looped around the elephant's neck, and he let out a soft moan as his head jerked forward. For the first time, Smalls noticed the thick chains wrapped around the elephant's ankles. They dug into his skin, making his gait slow and wobbly.

Lloyd threw open the door to the largest cage, and Loyd pulled the elephant toward it. But just outside the cage, the elephant stopped, refusing to take another step. Loyd yanked impatiently at the rope. "I said no shenanigans," he snapped.

But still the elephant didn't move. He just swung his trunk back and forth, looking nervous. "What do you think, Loyd?" Lloyd asked loudly. "Should we get Claude's *little friend*?"

The instant the words were out of Lloyd's mouth, the elephant's whole body sagged. His head drooped and his ears flapped and his trunk slumped against the ground. This time, when Loyd pulled the elephant toward the cage, he slunk inside.

"Nicely done, Lloyd," Loyd said.

"Nicely done, Loyd," Lloyd echoed. They walked out of the caravan, letting the door slam shut behind them.

In the silence they left behind, Smalls, Tilda, Wombat, and Rigby all stared at the elephant. The elephant stared back at them. Finally, Wombat stepped to the front of his cage, sticking his snout between the bars. "Greetings," he ventured, nodding politely at the elephant. "How do you do?"

"How do I *do*?" the elephant scoffed. His voice was low

and raspy. "Where didya come from? The 1800s?" He narrowed his eyes at the animals. "If you really wanna know, I think I *do* about as well as you all *look*." With a chuckle, he held up his trunk and rubbed the smear of peanut butter onto the wall of his cage. Then he sucked it off, slurping it down loudly. On the other side of the caravan, Rigby's stomach let out a hungry growl.

Clearing his throat, Wombat tried again. "I'm Wombat," he said. "But my friends call me Fred."

The elephant sneered at him. "I think I'll stick with Wombat."

"And may I ask what your name is?" Wombat pressed.

The elephant waved his trunk dismissively through the air. "If ya want."

When the elephant didn't elaborate, Wombat took a deep breath. "Okay," he said through gritted teeth. "What is your name?"

"I'm Lord Jest," the elephant said. "*Lord* Jest," he clarified. "Never just Jest."

"Nice to meet you, Lord Jest," Tilda offered, using her sweetest voice. "I'm Tilda, and the others are Smalls and Rigby."

Lord Jest shook his head, looking annoyed. "A prissy rabbit, a boring dog, a measly wombat, and a bear so small he could be a kitten. How does Claude think misfits like *you* are gonna spice up the circus?"

"Going to," Wombat corrected automatically, at the same time Smalls said, "*Circus?*"

Smalls reared up so fast he banged his head into the ceiling. "What do you mean by *circus?*"

"You mean no one told ya?" Lord Jest let out a harsh laugh. "I guess I get the pleasure." He looked from Smalls to Wombat to Tilda to Rigby. "Welcome, *Misfits*, to the Most Magnificent Traveling Circus. I think you're just gonna love it here."

Chapter Thirteen

A New Act

"**H**oly horseshoe," Smalls said, rubbing absently at the yellow horseshoe on his chest. "We're at the circus." He'd never been to a circus, but the word made him think of surprises, of clowns and laughter and things that shouldn't be, couldn't be, but somehow were. *And animals.* The thought struck him suddenly. Weren't there animals in a circus?

"The circus?" Rigby asked excitedly. "I've always wanted to watch a circus!"

"Watch?" Lord Jest let out an amused honk. "There will be no watching for you. You'll be *performing.* You're the new act at the circus, Misfits."

Rigby shook the fur out of his eyes. "What's an act?" he asked slowly.

Lord Jest snorted. "Wow, ya musta lived in a *cave* before this." He snaked his long, gray trunk through the bars of the cage, swinging it back and forth in front of the Misfits. "An act means you're performers. Ya do tricks and stuff for the crowd."

Smalls bolted upright in his cage, his heart beating fast. There *were* animals in the circus. And they were about to be them.

"Which is really a joke when ya think aboudit," Lord Jest continued in his gravelly voice. "Since you'll never compare to us Lifers."

"Lifers?" Tilda squeaked. She was nibbling furiously at her paws, removing any stray bits of burrs or dirt that had gotten caught there during the drive.

"Yeah, *Lifers*," Lord Jest said. "You a parrot or a rabbit? We Lifers are the *real* circus performers. Born and raised. There's Buck the zebra, May the monkey, the two lions, Hamlet and Juliet, and then there's me. The main act." Lord Jest gave his trunk an angry swish. "You get that through your heads, okay? *I'm* the star. I've been here longer than any of the other animals, even old May. Which means *I* get the rewards. Got me?"

The animals were saved from answering by the sound of the door swinging open. Fresh air poured inside, washing over Smalls. He tensed as he waited to hear Lloyd and Loyd's heavy footsteps, but this time, the footsteps were different. Two sets: one firm and sturdy, the other soft and nimble.

"Close the door!" a man's voice scolded. Smalls recognized the sharp, nasal voice immediately. It belonged to Claude, the man in the top hat.

"But it's so hot in here, Uncle," a boy's voice responded. "And if I'm hot, think about how the animals must feel—"

"How many times do I have to tell you, boy?" Claude interrupted as he came into Smalls's view. "Animals don't have feelings. It's a scientific fact." Raising a large silver jug to his lips, Claude took a long swig. Steam wafted off the jug, filling the caravan with a rich, sweet smell as it curled to the ceiling.

Smalls took a deep breath, wanting to suck in that sweetness, swallow it down. But suddenly it was drowned out by a different smell—a soggy, curdled, rancid smell that made something turn in Smalls's stomach. The boy emerged from behind Claude, gripping a tall stack of wooden trays in his hands.

The terrible smell was pouring off those trays in waves, but Smalls barely noticed it anymore. Because the boy standing before him was the one from the black motorcar, the one whose bright blue eyes had stared out at him through the window. Bertie.

For the first time, Smalls got a full view of him. He was skinny, all knobby knees and elbows and wrists, and his

baseball cap kept slipping down his forehead. His freckles made Smalls think of stars, how if you traced from one to another, you could find a constellation. The boy's white shirt was worn thin in several spots, and his brown pants were held up by a pair of old red suspenders. The pants were so short, you could see his skinny ankles above his mismatched shoes, and Smalls's eyes widened as he noticed an angry red welt spreading across his skin.

Next to Bertie, Claude swilled from his jug, then smacked his lips loudly. "Get to work, boy," he snapped, without bothering to look up.

Smalls watched as Bertie's hands tightened around the trays, turning his knuckles white. "Yes, Uncle," he said through gritted teeth.

Yes, Uncle, yes, Uncle, yes, Uncle. It seemed like Bertie could go through entire days uttering only those two awful words. Sometimes he dreamed about what it would be like to say no, just once. *NO!* He imagined how the word would shoot out of his mouth like a bullet, ricocheting through the air.

Taking a deep breath, Bertie walked over to Lord Jest's cage, sliding a tray under the bars. There was a pile of thick, slimy, crusty brown slop on top of it, and Bertie grimaced as he remembered the time he was forced to eat it. Claude had run out of the dry oats that made up Bertie's breakfast, lunch, and dinner, leaving Bertie with only one option to fill his empty, growling stomach: the animals' slop. It had been awful, as crunchy as it was slimy, sticking to the roof of his mouth no matter how many times he swallowed. And the taste! It had tasted like dead frogs, Bertie remembered, like rotten, decaying, slimy frogs, slinking down his throat and into his stomach.

In his cage, Lord Jest eyed the tray warily. "Sorry, Lord Jest," Bertie whispered.

Claude, who had taken a break from his cocoa to gnaw on a pinky nail, looked up sharply at the sound of Bertie's voice. He spit the fingernail out. It tumbled to the ground, bouncing off his shiny red shoe. "There is no *conversing* with the animals. You know I require absolute silence to drink my cocoa. Can you manage that, you worthless boy?"

Bertie stood back up, counting slowly to ten in his mind. It was what he did whenever that dangerous word—*NO*—began to rise inside him, threatening to escape. He paused, waiting until the word was safely locked away again: trapped behind bars and sealed in a box and buried deep in his stomach. Only then did he say, "Yes, Uncle."

Once, he'd come close to saying no. His uncle had ordered him to skip the animals' dinner for the night, and instead of saying *Yes, Uncle,* he'd asked, *Are you sure?* For several long seconds, his uncle had stared at him, his eyes cold and emotionless. Then he'd made Lloyd and Loyd pick Bertie up and toss him into a tiny cabinet in the back of the supply caravan. "This," he'd said, "is what happens to boys who talk back to me."

Claude had locked Bertie in that cabinet for two days, his knees jammed into his chest and his chin between his legs and his back stooped into a curve. It had been so dark in there he couldn't see his own hands and so hot that sweat had trickled down his arms and pooled behind his ears, making him feel feverish and chilled at the very same time. Late at night, something warm and furry had brushed against his skin and nipped at his ankles, but no matter how loud Bertie screamed, no one had let him out.

His last few hours in that cabinet, he'd been so dizzy from thirst and hunger and pain that the walls had seemed to spin around him like a carousel. When his uncle finally let him out, his legs were so dead asleep that he'd collapsed onto the floor, unable to use them. In that moment, with the rough floor against his cheek and his stomach as hollow as a tunnel, Bertie had made himself a promise. As long as he was living with his uncle, he would never, ever, *ever* say no.

Bertie kept counting in his head as he moved on to the

cages of the new animals. The dog was in the first one. He shook several tufts of white fur out of his eyes as Bertie slid him the tray. Rigby was his name, Bertie knew. He'd read that article about the Misfits a million times by now, memorizing every single word. He knew how Rigby played "mop" and Wombat expertly burrowed and Tilda could be mistaken for a cloud. And of course, how Smalls had traveled all the way from Asia when he was just a cub.

Bertie moved on, slipping a tray into Tilda's cage. She hopped briskly away from it, her tiny black nose quivering. Sighing, he gave a tray to Wombat, who nosed it curiously with his furry, brown snout. Bertie paused when he reached the last cage. *He looks . . . stately,* Bertie decided as he peered in at Smalls. The bear was sitting on his haunches, staring right back at him.

He looks . . . sad, Smalls thought as Bertie slid the sour-smelling tray into his cage. *Like he needs to play.* Smalls imagined Bertie throwing a ball to him. His muscles would tighten and release as he galloped after it, catching it smoothly on his tongue. He'd wing it back through the air and Bertie would smile as he chased after it, his skinny legs kicking up behind him. *I bet he has a nice smile,* Smalls thought, and instantly a list began to take shape in his mind. *Ways to Make Bertie Smile.*

"Boy!" Claude barked. Bertie's heart leapt into his throat as he whirled around to face his uncle. Sometimes Bertie worried that Claude could read his mind, that somehow he would *know* when Bertie was thinking nice thoughts about the animals. "Don't keep me waiting," Claude snapped. He took a final swig of his cocoa, tapping the bottom of the jug to get every last drop. Then he grabbed Bertie by the nose. "Come on." Pinching hard, he dragged him out of the caravan.

Chapter Fourteen

The Fairy Tale's Over

Smalls stared down at his tray of slop. His stomach felt dark and cavernous, like a black hole. The only thing that could satisfy him right now was a nice, big bowl of warmed honey. And this looked nothing like honey.

Tilda took one sniff of her slop and looked haughtily away. "I can't eat that," she declared.

"Probably a good idea," Lord Jest agreed. "Who knows what's in there? Maybe even *rabbit*." Tilda let out a scandalized gasp. "Why dontcha just fling it my way?" Lord Jest continued. "Get that stink outta your cage?"

"So this is really it?" Wombat cut in before Tilda could answer Lord Jest. He peered down at the slop in dismay. "This is our evening meal?"

"Evening meal?" Lord Jest burst out laughing. "I don't know what fairy tale you all came from, but in *this* world, we don't get no evening meals."

"Don't get any," Wombat corrected.

"'Scuse me?" Glowering at Wombat, Lord Jest stomped one of his chained hooves against the floor. The whole caravan shook under its weight. Some of Tilda's slop spilled off her plate, and she let out a soft squeal, skittering away from it. "You wanna correct me again?" Lord Jest snarled.

Wombat snapped his mouth shut, looking shaken.

"As I was *saying*," Lord Jest continued. "We don't get no precious *evening meals* here. We get slop. Real food is earned, by the best performers. And like I said before, that's always me. So if you don't eat up, Misfits, I will. Because morning is a long ways away."

"I can't do it," Tilda said, shaking out her fur. "I'm just going to wait until Mumford comes to find us."

Smalls reached up to touch his four-leaf clovers, forgetting they were gone. The problem was, he knew what the others didn't. Mumford wasn't coming for them. He was the one who'd lost them in the first place. Smalls looked down at his slop. The edges were yellowing and there was a crust along the top. It looked about as appetizing as a bowl of wet, wiggling worms. But if he didn't want to starve, he'd have to eat it; they all would.

He lifted his head, mustering up his most cheerful

voice. "We," he announced, "are going to play a game." Smalls's mind began to race, ticking off a long list of possible games.

"Slop Pile Dodge?" Tilda asked hopefully, hopping even farther away from her tray.

"No, Imagine That Squirrel," Rigby argued.

That gave Smalls an idea. "This is a little like Imagine That Squirrel," he said. He walked to the edge of his cage, sticking his nose through the bars. He'd feel so much better if he could just see his friends! But the bars made it impossible. In the cage next to his, Wombat stuck his snout out, and out of the corners of Smalls's eyes, he could just make out its furry brown tip.

"I could use a game to divert my attention from that revolting tray," Wombat said.

"*Divert?*" Lord Jest mimicked from the across the way. "Who do ya think ya *are?*"

"I think that I am Fred," Wombat replied huffily. "A wombat of the rare and prestigious hairy-nosed variety." He lifted his snout proudly into the air. "Now tell us about this game, Smalls."

"I call it Delicious Dinner Dream," Smalls said. "We are each going to dream up the most delicious dinner possible! And as we eat our slop, we'll pretend it's transforming into our dream meal." He sat back, pleased with his game. "I'll start."

Closing his eyes, he pictured the most delicious dinner he could imagine. "Before me is a bowl of the sweetest, thickest, stickiest honey in the world." Smalls took a big slurp, imagining the way the honey would warm his stomach as he swallowed it down.

In the cage next to his, Wombat stuck his snout into his slop. "Alphabet stew," he murmured.

"A carrot feast," Tilda tried out. "Carrot cake and carrot soup and carrot pudding!" She took a tentative nibble and then another.

In the cage closest to the door, Rigby let his fur flop over his eyes. "An ice cream sundae," he imagined. "With ice cream in every color of the rainbow, scoops of pink and copper and violet . . ." He lowered his head, lapping up his slop in a single breath.

"Wow," Lord Jest said dryly. He looked up from his tray, which he'd already licked clean. "If it ain't a bunch of little princesses."

Smalls ignored him. Finishing up his meal, he sat back, listening in satisfaction to the sounds of slurping and chomping ringing through the air. Delicious Dinner Dream. It wasn't his favorite game, but it had done the trick.

A half hour later, with their stomachs full of mystery slop, the animals all began to yawn. "I think I'm just going to close my eyes . . ." Rigby murmured. The instant his head hit his paws, he was out, his snores blasting through the caravan.

"Wombat?" Smalls whispered. But Wombat's breathing had begun to deepen and lengthen. He too was fast asleep.

Smalls shifted in his cage. He was exhausted, the kind of tired that seeped into his bones and weighed him down, like he was filled with sand. But he just couldn't seem to get comfortable. When he rested his head on his paws, his back hit up against the wall. When he curled up against the wall, his paws slid into the bars. And when he tried to stretch out like he did at home, all four paws ended up smushed into the corners of his cage.

"Good luck with that," Lord Jest snorted. Smalls looked up to see Lord Jest watching him in amusement. He was standing in the middle of his cage, his head dipped slightly so as not to hit the ceiling. For a second, Smalls wished he could sleep standing up like an elephant.

"I'm fine," Smalls said coolly. He was quickly coming to the conclusion that he did not like Lord Jest. "But where are the other animals?" It was getting late, and still the other cages sat empty and unlocked.

"They didn't do so good at practice today." Lord Jest

smirked. "So Claude made them stay for a night practice with the Lloyds. Better get ready for that. I gotta feeling you're gonna have plenty of night practices of your own."

With a sigh, Smalls dropped his head onto his paws, trying to ignore the way his back jutted into the wall. All he wanted was to fall into a deep sleep and dream his way back to Mumford's. Slowly, his eyes drifted shut. In his mind he could see the farm, the way it always seemed cloaked in velvet at night, darkness wrapping around him like a cocoon. And then he was there: stretched out in his favorite oak tree, the leaves soft under his head and the smell of apples filling the air . . .

"Who do we have *here*?" An unfamiliar voice shook Smalls awake.

The other animals must have come back from their night practice, Smalls realized groggily. He kept his eyes squeezed shut, pretending to be asleep. He was much too tired for any more introductions.

"Why *hello*, sweet thing," the voice went on. It made several loud kissing noises. "I've been waiting for you my whole life."

"She's asleep, Buck," another unfamiliar voice, this one female, said sternly. "Plus, she's a *rabbit*."

"Yeah and you're a zebra," a third voice chimed in. "Isn't that against the natural order or something?"

The animals kept talking, but with his eyes closed tight, Smalls began to drift off again. Before he knew it, their voices were fading into nothingness and, in his dreams, Smalls was back on Mumford's farm, the moon glowing above him like a night-light.

Chapter Fifteen

A Thumping Tail

Bertie stifled a yawn as Claude dragged him away from the animals' caravan. They'd just led the Lifers back in from their night practice, and Bertie was more than ready to climb into bed and dream the whole world away. Then tomorrow, he could see Smalls again. The thought made his lips curve up in a smile—just as Claude looked over at him. He quickly wiped the smile off his face, but it was too late.

"Are you *smiling*?" Claude spit out. "How many times do I have to tell you? There is nothing worse than a happy boy. Now go clean the Big Top for tomorrow's practice." He gave Bertie's nose a hard yank, dragging him toward the red tent billowing in the distance. It was dark and still now, but Bertie knew that on show night, it would light up like a thousand stars. "I want it to be sparkling clean by morning."

Bertie stifled another yawn. His eyelids felt heavy, like

Lord Jest was standing on top of them. "By morning?" he repeated.

"That's what I said," Claude snapped. He adjusted his top hat, looking satisfied. "Now stop wasting my time and get to work!" He gave Bertie a rough shove, sending him stumbling forward. He landed on his knees in the dusty ground. "Worthless boy," Bertie heard Claude mutter as he stalked off toward his caravan.

Bertie grumbled under his breath as he pulled himself back up, brushing the dirt off his hands and knees. Forget Invisible Boy, he decided. He would be Invincible Boy: so strong he could lift cars and break open cages and send Claude crashing to *his* knees. "Invincible Boy to the rescue!" he tried out as he headed toward the Big Top. He imagined lifting Claude with a single hand and chucking him into the air like he was nothing but a rag doll. This time, when a smile crept onto his face, he didn't bother wiping it off.

Bertie was so caught up in his thoughts that he didn't notice the soft *whoosh*ing sound drifting out of the Big Top. "Invincible Boy Saves Family from Burning House!" he murmured to himself, imagining the newspaper articles he would spawn. "Invincible Boy Rescues Kitten from Very Tall Tree!" he continued, pulling open the door to the Big Top. "Invincible Boy Locks Claude Magnificence Up in a Cage!"

His smile widened at that one, but as he stepped into the tent, it quickly faltered. Because there, in the ring, letting out a *whoosh* as it sliced through the air, was the acrobatic rope. And swinging from the top of it was Susan.

As the rope whipped around the edge of the ring, Susan gripped it with her toes and ever so slowly released her hands. Soon she was soaring upside down through the air, held to the rope by only her legs. Bertie sucked in a breath. It didn't matter how many times he'd seen Susan perform in the past six months; it still amazed him. With her back arched and her arms spread wide and her long, blond hair fanning out behind her, Bertie thought she looked like a bird, like at any moment, she could spread her wings and fly.

Bertie knew he should turn, look away, *run*—return to clean after she'd left. Claude had made it abundantly clear that Bertie was to have nothing to do with Susan unless Claude specifically ordered it. But he couldn't seem to tear his eyes away. He watched as Susan lifted her hands and gripped the rope. She began twirling her way down it, faster and faster, until it looked like the rope was a part of her, just another arm or leg. Unable to stop himself, Bertie took a step closer. And then another. He would have taken another too, but at that second, Susan looked down.

She froze on the rope, stopping mid-twirl. Bertie opened

his mouth, but before he could say anything, an image of that cabinet flashed through his mind—so dark and cramped and sweltering—the very place he'd end up if Claude ever found out he'd spoken to Susan behind his back. The thought filled him with an icy terror, and suddenly he found himself snapping his mouth shut. Turning on his heels, he ran out of the tent.

Susan shook her head as she watched Bertie retreating from the Big Top. With a sigh, she jumped down from the rope, not bothering to finish her twirling. She'd thought Bertie was actually, *finally* going to say something to her. But apparently not. She'd been at the circus for six months now, and in all that time he hadn't uttered a single word to her. By the way he acted around her or, more accurately, *avoided* her, you would have thought she had the bubonic plague.

And he wasn't the only one who seemed to feel that way. The foreign family of tumblers she shared a sleeping caravan with—the five Nilling cousins—had made it abundantly clear how little they liked living with a ten-year-old girl. They wouldn't admit it out loud, of course, but she was positive that the scorpion she'd found under her pajamas and the manure that had made its way into her sheets were their way of trying to force her out. Sometimes they'd talk late into the night in their own language, throwing shoes at her curtain just to keep her awake. It all made Susan wonder if she had some kind of sign plastered to her forehead in flashing neon lights. I'M AN ALIEN, maybe. Or better yet: I'M CONTAGIOUS!

She flinched slightly as she wrapped an old piece of gauze around her rope-burned hands. Seeing Bertie had made her feel all antsy, like she'd just downed three colas. Ever since she'd come to the circus to work off her parents' debt to the Magnificence family, all she'd wanted was someone to talk to. She was sure she would have heard from her parents by now, but she hadn't received a single phone call or letter. "I wouldn't get your hopes up," Claude scoffed any time she asked him. "They were chomping at the bit to get rid of you. I doubt you'll ever hear from them again."

Susan pulled the gauze even tighter, ignoring the pain. There was only one thing that helped when she was feeling like this. She went over to the long rows of seats that surrounded the ring, crouching down to pull out her paint set from where she'd hidden it earlier. That paint set was the only thing she'd managed to take with her from her old home; she'd snuck it out under her jacket, where Claude couldn't see it. She shuddered whenever she thought about what Claude would do if he found her with it. But she refused to let it stop her. She'd rather eat cockroaches than not be able to paint.

Clutching the tin to her chest, she took off for the woods that bordered the circus grounds. Soon after arriving at the circus, she'd quickly realized that the best way to paint was to get out from under Claude's watchful eyes. So she'd begun sneaking away at every venue they stopped at, finding secret places to paint in peace. She'd found her best spot yet here: a cave not far from the edge of the woods. Its tall, smooth walls were the palest shade of gray, perfect for painting.

She'd loved going to that cave these past few days. Like most circus venues, this one was a dry, barren stretch of land, filled with pock holes and ditches, the type of place where dust settled over everything like ash. Nothing grew on land like that. But by the cave in the woods, everything changed. The ground became softer and smoother, and the air took on the dewy smell of wild grass and fresh flowers.

Susan moved quietly down the long line of caravans, keeping her head low. The last thing she needed was for Claude to find her wandering around and assign her some atrocious task, like emptying the caravans' toilets. Her dinner of dry oats rose in her throat as she remembered the last time she had to do that, how the stench had seemed to follow her around for days. She picked up her pace. But halfway down the line of caravans, a strange noise made her stop short.

It was a bark, coming from the animals' cages.

She thought quickly of all the animals in the circus. They hooted and growled and trumpeted and brayed, but not one of them *barked*. Susan's heart gave a thump. Her whole life she'd wanted a dog, but it was never something her parents could afford. Another bark drifted out from the caravan, this one a little louder.

Susan glanced quickly around. The circus grounds were quiet and still. Before she could talk herself out of it, she hurried over to the caravan. Standing on her tippy toes, she grabbed onto the bars of the window, pulling herself up. It was the only good thing about the ropes: they'd made her stronger than she'd ever been. Pressing her forehead against the bars, she peered inside.

There, locked up in the row of cages across from the Lifers, were four new animals: a bear, a rabbit, some kind of extra-large-looking guinea pig, and a dog. Her chest squeezed tighter as the dog looked up at her. His wide brown eyes peeked out from a mass of white fur as he tilted his head to the side. She couldn't help but smile at the inquisitive look in his eyes. Immediately, his tail began thumping softly against the floor.

SLAM!

The sound of a door shutting in the distance made Susan's breath catch in her throat. With one last glance at the dog, she let go of the bars, dropping easily to the ground. But as she took off at a sprint for the woods, she couldn't shake the image of that dog and his thumping tail.

Chapter Sixteen

A Very, Very, Very Large Number

Claude sat at the table in his caravan, staring longingly into an empty silver jug. Behind the jug was a tall ceramic urn, and every few seconds his eyes would flit over to it. "Just one more glass," he said finally. Smiling to himself, he grabbed the urn and spooned three scoops of cocoa powder into his jug, mixing in hot water. "Ahhh," he murmured as he lifted it to his lips.

The jug must have been ornate once, made of hammered silver with a handle covered in glittering red stones. But the years hadn't treated it well, and now the silver was dented and tarnished, the stones dulled and chipped. Everything in Claude's caravan was like that, from the carved wooden table that was now splotched with cocoa stains, to the green velvet couch that must have been truly elegant before the cushions began to rip, to the silk bedding in his sleeping compartment that would have been lavish if it hadn't worn thin in so many spots. Even Claude's letter opener must have been beautiful once: made of the finest jade. But it was now so scratched and nicked, he barely afforded it a glance as he lifted it off a thick stack of mail.

"Let's see who wrote to Claude Magnificence this week," he murmured to himself. "Magazine . . . magazine . . . magazine." He tossed three magazines into a wrought iron basket by the door. One by one, they landed on top of each other: *Circus Today, Circus Digest, Better Circuses & Plays.* "Ad . . . ad . . . ad." With a smirk, he tossed three glossy envelopes into the garbage.

The next envelope he came upon was different: smaller, dirtier, with a name written across the front in shaky handwriting. *Susan Ward.* He let out an annoyed grunt, tossing it aside. "Ooh, catalog," he said, turning back to the pile of mail. "Now *that* I want." He grabbed at it eagerly. "'Order here for all your cocoa needs,'" he read out loud. He stroked his white beard thoughtfully. "I do have a lot of cocoa needs." Leaning back in his chair, he began to flip through the catalog, letting out murmurs of exclamation as he dog-eared page after page.

He was so entranced by his cocoa catalog that he almost didn't notice the final envelope sitting on the table. It was creamy white and thick, something bulging inside. It was only when he reached for his urn for a third helping of cocoa that he saw it. With a sigh, he dropped the catalog, picking up the envelope instead.

Inside was a scroll of paper. He furrowed his brow as he unrolled it—and unrolled it and unrolled it. By the time he was done, the bottom of the scroll was resting on the floor. Printed on it was some kind of list. *BILL,* it said at the top, in bold black letters. Claude's eyes widened as they ran down the list. Finally he reached the bottom. There, printed in red, was a very, very, very large number.

Claude let out a gasp, dropping the scroll on the floor. "This can't be," he sputtered. He stood up, pacing across the length of his caravan. "I don't have debts like this! I *collect* debts like this." But every time he passed by the scroll, he would peek down at it, and that same number would stare back up at him.

He walked by the scroll once more. "Still there," he muttered. Pulling off his top hat, he hugged it to his chest as he gazed down at the number for several long minutes. "Well, I guess it's time then," he said finally, a strange note in his voice. Carefully, he placed his top hat back onto his head, adjusting it so it sat just so. Squaring his shoulders, he stalked over to the phone. For a second he hesitated, his hand hovering over the mouthpiece. But then he took a deep breath and picked it up, quickly dialing a number.

"Ames?" he said into the phone. "It's Claude Magnificence. Remember that deal we talked about? Well, I'm ready to consider it. Come to our next performance, and we'll talk." With a click, he hung up.

Meanwhile, in a different caravan, Lloyd, Loyd, and the circus's clowns were waking for the day. As they grumbled and groaned, banging elbows and heads climbing out of their bunk beds, Bertie slept on in the closet behind them.

Bertie was dreaming. In his dream he was a brave hero, fighting pirates on the high seas to rescue a blond-haired maiden. He was tall and he was strong and he said no all he wanted, shouting it out for the whole world to hear: "NO, NO, NO!" But as sunlight oozed in through the tiny slit of a window above his bed, Bertie's dream began to fade and break apart. He squeezed his eyes shut tighter, fighting to hold on to it. *I'm not ready,* he thought. Nights were his favorite time. In his dreams there was no circus, there was no Claude, there was no *yes, yes, yes.* In his dreams he could be anyone, even a hero.

"What are you doing, you worthless boy?" Claude's nasal voice floated into Bertie's room, and the last of Bertie's dream

shattered into pieces. Just like that, reality sank back in. He wasn't a hero on the high seas; he was in his closet bedroom, curled up on the old, burlap sack of straw that was his bed.

Bertie scrambled to his feet as Claude stormed into his room. But it didn't matter. Claude had caught him lounging. Claude was wearing one of his typical outfits, green today: shiny green shoes, green pants made of brushed velvet, a tight green vest with green buttons that looked ready to pop at any second, a green topcoat, and of course a green top hat, with green sequins around its brim.

Bertie's room was so small that he and Claude had no choice but to stand nose to nose in it. "I didn't realize it was nap time," Claude said. Bertie's fists clenched at his sides as he smelled the cocoa on Claude's breath. When Bertie first came to live with his uncle after his dad died, he'd asked if he too could have a jug of cocoa in the morning. Claude had laughed so hard his face had turned purple. "You," he'd told Bertie, "are not worth the *hot water* I mix my cocoa with."

"We have our first training session with the new animals today," Claude continued. "And there will be a very important guest at our next show." Claude chewed on one of his fingernails, spitting it out in Bertie's face. "So hurry up and get dressed, boy." With a swish of his green coattails, Claude stormed out.

Bertie waited until he was gone to scoop up the fingernail Claude had spit out. Holding it as far from his face as possible, he slipped it into the jar he kept hidden under his bed. He'd been collecting the fingernails for years now, every time Claude spit one out in his face. Soon the jar would be full, and when it was, Bertie had a plan. A tiny smile tugged at his lips as he got dressed. One day, somehow, he was going to find a way to dump those nails into Claude's urn of cocoa powder. Then Claude could mix his precious hot water with *that*.

Chapter Seventeen

Wiped Clean

Claude's long, skinny legs moved fast, and Bertie had to jog to keep up as they made their way to the Big Top. Bertie cleared his throat. He had a question to ask his uncle, and he knew just how much his uncle hated his questions. "Uncle Claude?" he began.

"Hmm?" Claude murmured. He was mumbling to himself about money—probably what they'd make at their next show—and Bertie couldn't tell if he was even listening.

"I was wondering," Bertie continued, raising his voice to try to get his attention, "if you put my wages away for me this month?"

"Of course I did," Claude spit out. Under his breath, he muttered, "Seven hundred and ten dollars, seven hundred and thirty dollars, seven hundred and sixty dollars . . ."

"And do you think," Bertie pressed, "that one day soon

I'll have earned enough to visit my mom?"

Stopping short, Claude spun around, grabbing Bertie's shoulders. He shook them hard, his fingers digging into his skin. "Didn't I say I'd tell you when you had enough?" Claude snapped.

Bertie nodded. "Yes, but—"

"Then," Claude said coldly, cutting him off. "That's your answer." Pushing Bertie aside, he took off for the Big Top, his long legs kicking up dust behind him.

Bertie took a deep breath. *Yes, Uncle.* That was what he was supposed to say; he knew that. But Bertie had turned ten last month; that marked five years since he'd first gone on the road with the circus. And the longer he was there, the harder it became to stay quiet. If only he could remember more about his past! Then maybe he'd know the right questions to ask his uncle. But the accident that had stolen his dad from him had stolen Bertie's memories as well—wiped him clean.

He could summon just the vaguest images of his parents: his mom's long red braid, his dad's bright blue eyes, the way they would both ruffle his hair before bed. He barely even remembered the accident itself—just the heat and the way the fire had come out of nowhere, turning his world upside down and inside out and never the same again.

When he was about seven, Claude had finally told him the story of the accident. They'd been on a drive in Claude's brand-new motorcar: Claude, Bertie, and Bertie's father, who was Claude's brother. But halfway through the drive, something went wrong. The car began to hiss and shake, and suddenly they were veering off the road, straight into a tree. Bertie was thrown from the motorcar, his head smashing against the ground. Claude managed to get out, but Bertie's father was trapped. And then the car went up in flames.

When his dad died, something broke inside his mom, something that couldn't be put back together again. So Claude sent her off to that hospital, and then he took his circus—and Bertie—on the road. "You're just lucky you didn't wind up in an orphanage, boy," he liked to tell Bertie. "Little boys get eaten alive in orphanages."

Whenever Bertie asked about visiting his mom, Claude reminded him just how expensive it would be. "Maybe if you didn't waste so much time sleeping at night, you'd finally have enough money," he told him. So month after month, year after year, Bertie had worked until his hands blistered and his back ached. And still, he never had enough.

Throwing back his shoulders, Bertie jogged after Claude. "Uncle," he called out, refusing to let a tremble creep into his voice. "When *exactly* do you think it will be?"

Claude stopped in his tracks. Slowly, he turned around. This time, he didn't yell, he didn't grab Bertie, he didn't shake him. He just looked at him, his eyes cold and steely. "You are never," Claude said slowly, "*ever* to talk back to me." He took a step forward, closing the space between them. His hands were trembling at his sides. Bertie's heart began to pound. "Unless," Claude continued, "you'd like to spend a few more days in that cabinet. Understood?"

Bertie dropped his eyes. The memory of the cabinet surged through him like an electric shock, setting every one of his nerves on edge. "Yes, Uncle," he whispered.

"That's what I thought." Grabbing Bertie by the nose, Claude pulled him toward the Big Top. "Now hurry up, boy. You have work to do."

Chapter Eighteen
Rabbits Don't Wear Bows

Bertie counted to ten over and over in his head as Claude dragged him toward the Big Top, but the numbers did little to quell his anger. Five years was a long time not to see his mom. In five years he'd grown to twice his height, his freckles had multiplied, his red hair had darkened. Soon, she might not even recognize him anymore.

"Pick up the pace," Claude barked, giving Bertie's nose a hard yank. "We've got an important show coming up." Bertie wondered briefly what was so important about it, but he quickly brushed the thought aside. There was probably a purveyor of cocoa coming to the show, and Claude was hoping for a free refill for his urn. He counted silently to ten again, shoving his anger deep down inside him.

"No, no, no!" Claude's sharp tone made Bertie look up. Claude had his eyes trained on one of the caravans. Susan was out front, stretching in her shimmery blue leotard and skirt. "She's going to ruin her costume," Claude seethed. "And if she thinks I'm going to buy her another one . . . well, she is sorely mistaken." Pinching Bertie's nose, he dragged him toward Susan.

"What are you *doing*, girl?" he spat out when he reached her. Bertie could feel his cheeks heating up as Susan's light brown eyes traveled from him to Claude and back again.

"I just thought—" she began.

"Well, don't," Claude cut in. "I didn't bring you here to *think*. I brought you here to *perform*. Now go practice inside your caravan, where the dust and the dirt and the"—he cringed—"nature won't ruin your costume."

"Yes, Master Magnificence," Susan said softly. But she stared unflinchingly at Claude as she spoke, and Bertie got the sense she wished she was saying something else altogether. Bertie could feel his eyes crinkling up with the tiniest of smiles, and he quickly looked down at the ground before anyone could see it.

"Come on, boy." With a final glower in Susan's direction, Claude yanked Bertie toward the Big Top. But as Bertie stumbled after him, he couldn't help but glance over his shoulder, just in time to see Susan disappearing into her caravan.

● ● ●

Susan waited until the door to her caravan was firmly shut behind her before letting out a loud groan. It had taken all her strength not to kick *Master Magnificence* right in his velvet-covered shins. She wondered what Bertie would have done if she had. For a second, before he'd looked down, she could have sworn she'd seen a flash of amusement in his eyes, almost as if he'd known what she was thinking. But maybe it was just her imagination.

With another groan, she headed into her tiny sleeping compartment, pulling the curtain shut behind her. If Claude didn't want her practicing outside, then she wouldn't practice at all. Kneeling down, she reached under her burlap sack bed, feeling around for her paint set. Earlier today she'd found an almost completely clean napkin in the trash, and she'd been itching to paint on it ever since. But as she pulled her paint set out, it wasn't the napkin that came out with it. It was a photo, *the* photo, the one she'd found tucked away in the pocket of her coat on her very first night at the circus.

Susan blinked as she stared down at the square of paper. A man and a woman stared back at her. The man was smiling so wide you could see the tooth missing in the back of his mouth, and the woman was looking up at him with the same light brown eyes that Susan had, her blond hair tumbling over her shoulders. Susan shoved the photo of her parents back under her bed. Every time she looked at it, she could hear Claude's voice in her head. *They didn't want you anymore, Susan. Little girls are too expensive for poor farmers like your parents.*

Susan took a deep breath. Thinking about her parents, about home, made everything seem darker, like someone had taken a pen and colored over the sun. She reached back under the bed, fishing around for the napkin. There was only one way she knew to beat back that darkness. Opening the napkin on her lap, she pulled out her paintbrush. An image of that dog—Rigby, she'd heard one of the Lloyds call him— flashed through her mind. She knew exactly what she wanted to paint.

Over in the Big Top, Smalls, Rigby, Tilda, and Wombat were being led into the ring in chains. "That chain was ruining my fur," Tilda sulked as Lloyd freed her. She twisted her head around, trying to catch a glimpse of her back. "Be honest, Wombat. How bad is the damage?" Wombat just gave her a gentle nudge in response.

With a sigh, Smalls shook out his paws. Lloyd had wrapped the chains around them so tightly that pins and needles had started to prickle through his legs.

Over by the door, Loyd and Lloyd had their heads bent together. "You know what I've been wondering, Loyd?" Smalls heard Lloyd ask.

"I do know, Lloyd," Loyd replied solemnly. "Because I've been wondering it too. What exactly makes all these lights light up?"

Loyd and Lloyd looked up at the tent's ceiling, where thousands of tiny bright bulbs were strung. "Maybe they're actually bottled stars," Lloyd said thoughtfully.

"Or maybe," Loyd replied excitedly, "there's a firefly glowing inside every one of them!"

"Yes," Lloyd agreed. "That sounds exactly right." Suddenly, he blinked. "But that wasn't what I was wondering, Loyd."

Loyd scrunched up his forehead. "Then what, Lloyd?"

Lloyd walked over to Tilda. "I was wondering," he said, "what that red *thing* on top of the rabbit's head is."

Tilda looked up sharply. *"Thing?"* she sputtered. "That *thing* is my bow! Made of genuine red silk!" She looked over at Wombat, who was busy trying unsuccessfully to burrow a hole in the tent's velvet floor. "Tell them, Wombat."

"Genuine red silk," he agreed. "Found by yours truly in the apple orchard. And Tilda, it's Fred now."

"It looks like a bow," Loyd said, ignoring the squeaks

and grunts coming from Wombat and Tilda. "But rabbits don't wear bows!"

The twins looked at each other worriedly. "We should probably get rid of it before Boss sees," Lloyd said.

Bending down, Loyd tore the bow out of Tilda's fur. "There," he said, tossing it into a trash can next to the row of seats. "Problem solved."

"My bow!" Tilda screeched. As Wombat rushed to her side, Loyd and Lloyd smiled proudly at each other.

"What would Boss do without us?" Loyd asked.

"He'd be lost," Lloyd replied. "That's for sure."

Chapter Nineteen

Fire Sticks

Claude opened the door to the Big Top, shoving Bertie inside. Bertie rubbed at his nose as he stumbled forward. For a man whose most physical act of the day was lifting his jug of cocoa, Claude sure had a strong grip. Bertie glanced toward the ring to where the new animals were waiting. They were all gathered around Tilda the rabbit, who was squeaking loudly.

Claude grabbed his arm and began spitting out instructions. "We'll bring the Lifers in later, but let's focus on the new animals for now. They've got plenty to learn. Lloyd, you take the bear," he ordered. "Loyd, that leaves you with the rest of them. I, as always, will supervise."

As always, Bertie mimicked in his head. *Since I, Claudius Magnificence, would never dare lift a finger myself!*

"Did you say something, boy?" Claude asked, looking down at him coldly.

"No, Uncle," Bertie said quickly.

Claude narrowed his eyes at him. "Go get my little friend, Wilson," he snapped. "I left it in the supply caravan."

Bertie nodded, hurrying out of the Big Top. He blew out a long breath as Claude's voice faded into the distance. Up ahead, he could see the supply caravan. Just like all the other caravans, it had probably been magnificent once, red and shiny and gilded. But now it was caked in so much dust and dirt, it was nearly brown. A few feet down, the Nilling cousins were practicing their act on the dusty ground. One by one, they climbed onto each other's shoulders—until they'd built a human tower five Nillings high. Bertie paused, watching as the top Nilling flipped into the air, making three full rotations before landing gracefully on her feet.

Pushing his baseball cap off his forehead, Bertie climbed into the supply caravan. It was stuffed to the gills—filled with trapezes and curtains, stilts and tight ropes, tickets and juggling balls, hula hoops and unicycles, costumes and wigs—so it took him a minute to find Wilson. The stick looked like it always did: long and lean, the silver end shiny and curved. When Bertie first saw it, he'd thought it was a cane. Then he'd noticed the sharp tip at the very end.

Out of the corners of his eyes, Bertie could see that awful cabinet he'd spent days in, but he refused to look over at it.

Holding tightly to Wilson, he jumped down from the caravan and hurried back to the Big Top. But when he pulled the door to the tent open, he froze in place. In just a few minutes' time, the ring of the Big Top had turned into a disaster zone.

In the front of the ring, Loyd was trying to teach Tilda, Wombat, and Rigby their tricks all at once. But instead of balancing on a beach ball, Rigby flopped onto his stomach. Instead of walking across a tightrope, Wombat tumbled to the ground. And instead of leaping into a top hat, Tilda somehow landed underneath it. But that wasn't what drew a gasp from Bertie.

Sitting in the center of the ring was a hoop of fire. Lloyd was standing in front of it, holding six flaming sticks in his hands. "No," Bertie whispered. Claude couldn't be teaching the new animals to use fire sticks already! *Could he?* As Lloyd tossed one of the fire sticks into the air, Bertie got his answer.

"Go!" Lloyd shouted at Smalls. "Catch the stick with your tongue!" Bertie's heart sank as he watched Smalls. Instead of leaping through the hoop and catching the fire stick in his mouth, he just stood there, his head cocked to the side as he stared at Lloyd. The stick hit the ground with a crack, sparks flying everywhere.

"Worthless bear," Claude muttered, his face reddening. He paced along the edge of the ring, stroking furiously at his beard. Bertie's palms grew sticky as they clung tightly to Wilson. The stick was dangerous on Claude's best days. Thinking about what Claude might do with it now sent a cold shiver running down his spine.

Claude gnawed on a fingernail, spitting it out at Tilda, who had just managed to untangle herself from the top hat. It landed on her back, sinking instantly into her downy white fur. She let out a strangled squeal as she began frantically trying to shake it out. Ignoring her, Claude turned back to Lloyd. "Again," he ordered.

This time, Lloyd gave Smalls a hefty kick in the backside. With a growl, Smalls leapt forward, flying through the hoop. As Lloyd tossed the fire stick into the air above him, Smalls looked up, following it with his eyes. For a second, it looked like he might try to catch it. But as he landed on the ground, his back bumped against the hoop, setting a patch of fur on fire. Smalls howled wildly as he crashed to the ground, rolling back and forth to put out the flames. They'd just flickered out when the fire stick hurtled down on top of him, landing with a sizzle on his paw. Claude covered his ears as Smalls let out another howl.

Noticing Bertie for the first time, Claude waved him over. "What are you waiting for, boy? Bring me Wilson! Clearly this bear needs it."

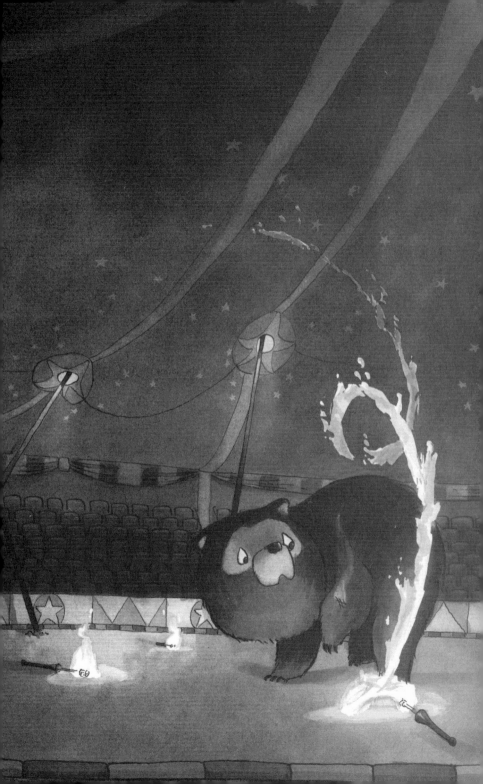

Bertie nodded. But his feet suddenly felt chained to the ground. As hard as he tried, he couldn't seem to move them. His uncle's voice rang out in his head. *Animals don't have feelings!* But when Bertie looked at Smalls, he was positive it wasn't just pain he saw in the bear's eyes, but sadness too.

Claude stalked over to Bertie. "Worthless," he muttered, grabbing the stick away from him. Twirling it in his hands, he turned back to Smalls. "Now, where were we?"

Chapter Twenty
A Sultry Wink

Smalls hurt all over. His tongue was hot and singed, his shoulders smarted from all the spills he'd taken, and his back throbbed from all his burns. He felt like an old machine whose parts were breaking down, one by one. But it was worth it because somehow he'd managed to avoid Wilson.

When Claude had grabbed that stick out of Bertie's hands, something inside Smalls, something old and ancient and wild, had told him he didn't want to see what that stick could do. So he'd done everything in his power to avoid it. He'd leapt. He'd jumped. He'd scrambled. He'd ignored the pain searing through his tongue and soared through the flames, catching fire stick after fire stick.

Now, as Claude ordered Bertie to get more equipment from the supply caravan and Lloyd and Loyd brought the Lifers in for their training, Smalls collapsed in the back of the ring, desperate for a break. Lord Jest came in first, the chains around his legs rattling as he lumbered into the ring. He shot Smalls and the others a nasty look as he passed them. The rest of the Lifers followed him, chained together in a single-file line. The lions, Hamlet and Juliet, were at the front. According to the brief introduction Smalls had gotten during their morning slop, Hamlet was the younger sibling, but he was larger, with thick paws and a dark, wild mane around his face. Juliet was fairer, with tawny muscles and silky fur the color of spun gold. Behind them was Buck, a zebra with snow-white hair and oily black stripes. Last came May, a thin, brown monkey with a hunched back and fur that had gone white around the nose.

As Lloyd and Loyd began unchaining the Lifers, Buck looked right at Tilda and lowered one of his eyelids in a sultry wink.

"Um, Tilda?" Wombat said slowly. At the sound of an *um* coming from Wombat's mouth, Smalls, Rigby, and Tilda all whipped around to look at him. It was a rare moment when Wombat was anything less than fastidious about his choice of words. "Did that zebra just *wink* at you?"

Tilda cleared her throat nervously. "I think?" she squeaked.

Wombat pawed angrily at the ground. "He winked at *my* girlfriend? *Mine?*"

Smalls cringed. The use of incomplete sentences was never a good sign either. "He probably just had some dust in his eye," Smalls assured him. He decided not to mention the *sweet thing* comment he'd overheard last night. "Right, Rigby?" He nudged Rigby to back him up.

"Absolutely," Rigby agreed. "He probably just . . ." He trailed off as a blue-winged butterfly flew past them. Brightening, he began to trot after it, his eyes glued to its wings. "It's so graceful," he breathed. He wiggled his shoulder blades, trying to imitate the butterfly. His long strands of fur flew from side to side, making him look like a mop cleaning the air. "Just look at how it glides . . ." Wiggling his shoulders even harder, Rigby crouched down low, trying to glide his way across the dusty ground. "I *am* a butterfly," he chanted to himself.

Lord Jest lifted his trunk, letting out a nasty honk. "They really are a ragtag lot, aren't they?" he snorted.

Juliet looked up from where she was helping May get settled in the corner. "Nothing for us to worry about," she agreed.

"Nothing to worry about at *all*," Buck replied, sidling up to Tilda. "Hi there, beautiful," he said, flashing her a hungry smile. "I like your fur." Moving closer to Tilda, he ran his black and white tail down her back.

"Pardon me!" Wombat exclaimed. He tried to butt in front of Buck, but Buck easily swatted him aside.

"You can't really be into that *rat*, can you?" Buck asked Tilda.

"For your information," Wombat seethed, "I am a rare and treasured hairy-nosed wombat. Descendant of the marsupials. Scientific name *Lasiorhinus latifrons*. I am *not* a rat. I am not even a commonplace regular-nosed Wombat! *Je suis un spectaculaire* hairy-nosed wombat!"

Buck ignored him. He had just started tickling Tilda's chin with the tip of his tail when Claude let out a sharp whistle. "Time for the Most Magnificent Traveling Circus's Original Animal Act!" he announced as Bertie returned to the Big Top. Bertie dragged a whole mound of supplies in with him, one after another: a huge wooden wheel and a colorful stool and a stack of hula hoops and a bag filled with juggling balls, hanging from the handlebar of a unicycle.

"Lloyds, get the animals set up," Claude ordered. "Bertie, I want you to go back to the supply caravan and write up tickets for the show." He paused, waiting for Bertie to deposit the last of the supplies in the ring. "And no rushing them! I want these to be the best tickets you've ever written up. Everything needs to be *perfect* for this show." He stroked his long white beard. "Understood?"

Smalls watched as Bertie looked down, refusing to meet his uncle's eyes. Several beads of sweat clung to his temples and he was breathing hard from carrying the supplies in. "Yes, Uncle," he said tersely.

As Bertie left the tent, Lord Jest sauntered past Smalls. "Watch and learn, buddy bear," he said, taking his place next to the colorful stool. "You're about to see how the real animals do it."

Chapter Twenty-one

Claude's Little Friend Is Your Worst Enemy

Right before Smalls's eyes, the Lifers transformed. Lord Jest stood upside down on a stool, balancing on his two front hooves. Using his trunk, he tossed ten colorful hoops into the air—one after another. As they fell back down, he curled his trunk so that each one slid smoothly onto it. Soon he was balanced upside down on two legs, with ten hoops dangling from his trunk like necklaces.

Nearby, Hamlet and Juliet mounted a huge wooden wheel, Hamlet inside and Juliet on top. They each galloped in place, Hamlet running in one direction and Juliet in the other, and slowly their strides began to roll the wheel around the ring, picking up speed as it went. Meanwhile, Buck juggled a dozen balls in the air using only his nose, and May circled him on a unicycle, pulling a never-ending chain of scarves out of a tiny black top hat.

"Holy horseshoe," Smalls murmured in awe. Back at Mumford's, he'd loved playing for the kids. But this was something else entirely.

"Faster, you lazy lions," Claude said. "Unless you're looking for a rendezvous with Wilson . . ." He waved his stick through the air and the lions ran even faster, their wheel spinning wildly around the ring. With a nod, Claude moved on to May, scrutinizing her hands as they slowly pedaled the unicycle forward. Unlike the other animals, who performed their tricks effortlessly, May was panting hard, her whitened face scrunched up in concentration as she pedaled with her hands and pulled scarves with her feet at the same time.

"Faster," Claude ordered her. May bent forward, her hunched back poking into the air. She picked up her speed, trembling with the effort. Her hands were shaking so badly that the tiny top hat slipped from her grip, sending a long chain of scarves flapping through the air. "What's wrong with the monkey?" Claude asked. He chewed on his pointer fingernail, spitting it out as he turned to Lloyd and Loyd.

"She's lazy?" Lloyd suggested.

"She's old?" Loyd offered.

Claude paced in a circle, stroking urgently at his beard. "I don't care if she's ancient! We have an important show coming up, and I need every animal to be perfect." He stopped in front of May. "Faster," he demanded.

May grunted, pedaling harder, but her breath was growing raspy and her whiskers were starting to droop and she was trembling harder than ever. The more she trembled, the more the unicycle wobbled, until she could barely keep upright.

"Faster!" Claude said again.

"This," May panted, "is as fast as this old monkey goes."

Claude cringed. "Stop that grunting and *move*. Or you'll move right into this." He waved Wilson at her.

May drew in a strangled breath, trying desperately to pedal faster. But instead, one of her feet slid off and suddenly she was flailing through the air. She landed on the ground with a terrible thud, her tail crunching under the wheel of the unicycle.

"You worthless monkey!" Claude shouted. Smalls watched in horror as Claude raised Wilson into the air, throwing it with all his might. It landed on the ground with a loud crash, narrowly missing May. "Come on, Lloyds," he snapped. "It's time for lunch. I'm ready for a break from this animal stench!" He stormed out of the Big Top with Lloyd and Loyd close on his heels.

The instant the humans were gone, Juliet rushed over to

May. "Are you all right?" she asked frantically. Crouching next to the monkey, she gave her a gentle nudge with her nose.

"I'm sure I'll be fine." May sighed. She had a soft, smooth voice that made Smalls think of the creek back at Mumford's, the way it used to trickle over the rocks. "I just got a little nick on my tail." With a soft groan, she took her tail in her hands and began nursing her wound.

"Do you think Claude's always like that?" Tilda whispered to Smalls.

Smalls blinked, unable to answer. He reached for a four-leaf clover for reassurance but found only fur behind his ear. He took a deep breath. He couldn't fall apart now! His friends needed him. Quickly, he ran through his happiest list in his head.

My Favorite Spots to Eat Honey

1. In a clump of wildflowers, bees buzzing all around me.

2. *Next to the creek, with the cool water lapping at my paws.*

3. *On the very top branch of my oak tree, so high up that the sun feels like it belongs to me.*

There. That was better. Clearing his throat, he looked down at Tilda. "I'm sure not *always*," he said, even though he wasn't sure at all.

Rigby let out a soft growl. "May was just lucky that awful stick missed her."

"Who gives a stick a name, anyway?" Wombat asked angrily. "It's an inanimate object, not a *friend*!"

In the back of the ring, Lord Jest let out a nasty laugh. "That's where you're wrong." He lumbered over to them, his hooves clapping against the ground like thunder. "That stick is like Claude's best friend. His *only* friend. Here, why dontcha take a look for yourself."

Lifting an old, leathery leg, Lord Jest displayed a thin pink scar running along its side. "This is from Wilson." He ducked his head, revealing another scar, this one thicker and pinker. "And so is this." Turning around, he revealed a third pink line on his back, long and slightly raised. "And, of course, this. And believe me, there's been more."

"But that's . . . abominable," Wombat whispered.

"No," Lord Jest corrected. "That's circus life. Around these parts, Claude's *little friend*, Wilson, is your worst enemy."

Chapter Twenty-two

The Finale of the Millennium

Claude returned from lunch with tomato sauce on his breath and a scowl on his face. Lloyd and Loyd were behind him, fighting over which of them had eaten more french fries. "But I had thirty-six and you only had thirty-five," Lloyd argued.

"Lloyd!" Claude barked. "Loyd!" The twins immediately fell silent. "I have news," Claude announced.

"Yes, Boss?" Lloyd pushed Loyd aside to get to Claude first.

"Yes, Boss?" Loyd glared at Lloyd as he shoved him back.

"I thought long and hard over lunch, and . . ." Claude held both hands up in the air, pausing dramatically.

"And?" Loyd asked eagerly.

"And?" Lloyd asked excitedly.

"And," Claude continued. "I have scripted a new finale for the circus!"

"Oh." Identical looks of disappointment flashed across the twins' faces.

"No promotion," Lloyd whispered to Loyd.

"No raise," Loyd whispered to Lloyd.

"It's going to be spectacular," Claude continued. "Just the thing we need to blow Ames—ahem, *everyone* away! And then," Claude went on, "when everything goes as planned, you two will get a nice, fat bonus."

"Great!" Lloyd exclaimed.

"Wonderful!" Loyd sang out.

"Now," Claude said, stroking his beard. "I sent Bertie to get Susan, who's going to be my secret weapon in the Most Magnificent Traveling Circus's new finale. So stop your bickering and make sure the animals are set up before she gets here."

"Of course, Boss," Lloyd said readily.

"Anything you need, Boss," Loyd said eagerly.

Claude smiled thinly. "That's what I like to hear."

On the other end of the circus grounds, Bertie was pacing back and forth outside Susan's caravan. "Hello, Susan," he practiced. He wrinkled his nose. Too formal. "Pardon me,

Susan," he tried again. That made him sound like an old man. He threw his arms into the air in frustration.

Why was he even thinking about this? Claude was always sending him off to fetch one performer or another. He never practiced his greetings for *them*. But ever since Claude had dragged him over to talk to Susan this morning, he hadn't been able to stop thinking about her. As he wrote out ticket after ticket in the supply caravan and choked down his bowl of dry oats at lunch, she kept sneaking her way back into his thoughts.

He just wished he hadn't sprinted away like such a coward when she caught him watching her on the rope last night. But this time was different. Claude had *ordered* him to talk to her. So what was he so worried about? He was just going to knock on the door and say—

"Bertie?"

Bertie whirled around to find Susan standing in the doorway of her caravan. Her long blond hair was pulled back in a ponytail, and there was a curious expression in her eyes.

"Claude sent me!" he burst out. His voice sounded funny, like there was a frog in his throat, and he coughed, trying to clear it. "He's created a new finale for the circus," he hurried on. "And he wants you to be in it. I think it just requires some simple acrobatics, but you're small enough that you can ride on the animals' backs, and of course you know how to do all the tumbling."

He was rambling, which was ridiculous, because he never rambled. But he couldn't seem to stop. "So do you want to do it? He wants you to come practice with us in the Big Top. I probably shouldn't even have asked if you want to since Claude didn't exactly ask. You know how he is when he gets an idea in his head . . ."

"He drinks cocoa and watches everyone else work on it?" The instant the words were out, Susan gasped, covering her mouth with her hand. "I—I didn't mean that," she swore through her fingers. "It came out wrong!" She stepped down from the caravan and suddenly she was only inches away from him. Up close, Bertie could see tiny flecks of green in her light brown eyes.

"Too bad," he said quietly. "Because that's exactly what he does." His heart skipped a beat. Had he really just said that? *Out loud?* He waited for the fear to slam into him, snatching his breath away and sending ice through his veins. But as Susan smiled tentatively at him, her green-brown eyes shining, he felt almost *good*. "Of course," he continued, glancing around to make sure no one else could hear, "he'd probably chew on his fingernails too."

"And then spit them out," Susan added solemnly.

"While stroking his beard," Bertie continued.

Susan reached up to stroke an imaginary beard. "Susan," she said, mimicking Claude's nasal whine. "I would like you to jump off a tower today. Of course it doesn't matter that the last person who did it died!"

Bertie burst out laughing. The sound felt foreign coming out of his mouth, but nice, like soda bubbling out of a fountain. "You sound just like him!"

Susan shrugged modestly. "I've been practicing. I can also do this." She pretended to chew vigorously on a fingernail, then spit it loudly in the direction of the Big Top.

"Uncanny," Bertie said. Laughter filled his stomach. *This must be what it's like to have a friend,* he thought.

Susan twirled a strand of blond hair around her finger. "Well, I guess we should get going," she said.

"Don't want to keep Claude Magnificence waiting," Bertie agreed.

"You know, I saw you last night," Susan said as they started for the Big Top. "You were watching me practice."

"I'm sorry." Bertie reached up nervously to adjust his baseball cap. "I wasn't spying, I swear. I just love the ropes. I could watch them forever."

"Well, I couldn't swing on them forever." Carefully, Susan unwrapped a piece of gauze from around one of her hands, holding it out for Bertie to see. There was a swarm of blisters on her palm, some white and hardened, others peeling and bleeding.

"Ow." Bertie flinched at the sight of dried blood smeared across her palm. "You should probably stay off the rope for a few days so those can heal."

"Ha!" Susan let out a bitter laugh. "Try telling your uncle that." Bertie fell silent. He had a feeling that would fall squarely in the *no* category. "I used to take ballet classes back home," Susan continued, "and whenever the blisters on my toes got too bad, my mom would make me skip class for a few days. But Claude isn't really the motherly type."

Bertie laughed. "You can say that again."

As they reached the Big Top, familiar sounds rose into the air around them: threats and grunts and growls and the telltale honk of an elephant. "Ready for a fingernail feast?" Susan whispered.

"Even better than ice cream," Bertie whispered back.

"Susan!" Claude exclaimed as Susan and Bertie walked into the ring. He reached up to stroke his beard, studying her through narrowed eyes. "How fine of you to join us."

As if she had a choice, Bertie thought.

"How would you like to be in the circus's brand-new finale?" Claude went on.

Susan forced a smile onto her face. "I'd love to, Master Magnificence," she gushed. *As if I have a choice,* she thought. Her eyes flickered to the back of the ring, where the new animals were huddled together. Rigby was pressed up against the bear, his face hidden beneath a thick mop of fur. As if he could sense her watching him, he looked up suddenly, his fur flapping out of his eyes. For a second, they just stared at each other, and even from across the ring, she could hear it: his tail thumping once, twice, three times against the floor.

"Wonderful," Claude said smoothly, drawing her attention back to him. "As long as these worthless Misfits learn their tricks, we'll have the finale of the *millennium* tomorrow."

"And of the century too!" Lloyd piped up.

"Even the decade!" Loyd chimed in.

In the back of the ring, Wombat growled under his breath. "And *we're* the stupid ones? It's absurd!"

Smalls nodded absently, but he wasn't paying attention. He was too busy thinking about the word Claude had used. *Tomorrow.*

Smalls's fur stood on end. In just one day, they'd be performing in the circus.

Chapter Twenty-three

A Sun Bear with a Useless Tongue

Walking to the front of the ring, Claude lifted his arms in the air as if he were conducting an orchestra. "Introducing the finale of the millennium," he announced. Then he began to shout out commands.

Instantly, the ring came alive with activity. Lord Jest kneeled on the ground, allowing Susan to mount his back. Then he climbed onto the stool, balancing on his front hooves as he used his trunk to toss up hoop after hoop. Each one flipped through the air before landing smoothly around Susan's waist. Such accurate tossing wasn't easy; it took precise calculations and complete concentration. But Lord Jest nailed it every time.

In the center of the ring, Hamlet and Juliet climbed onto their wheel and began spinning it toward Lord Jest. Lowering his head, Lord Jest stretched out his trunk. When the lions reached him, Susan slid down it like a slide. She landed on Juliet's back and rode sidesaddle as the lions rolled faster and faster. When they passed Buck, he began to gallop next to them, using his inky black nose to juggle twelve balls at once. Meanwhile, May leapt onto her unicycle, letting out a soft whimper as her wounded tail hit one of the spokes.

"Now!" Claude yelled. In the center of the ring, Loyd scooped up Wombat, placing him at the end of a tightrope held taut between Lloyd and Bertie.

Here was what was supposed to happen next:

Wombat was to use his strong legs to walk across the tightrope. When he reached the other end of the rope, Rigby—who had been waiting with a beach ball, his face and paws concealed beneath his fur—was to leap to his feet in a jack-in-the-box moment of surprise, balancing perfectly atop the ball. In his teeth would be six unlit fire sticks. Susan would then jump down from Juliet's back to light the fire sticks and toss them one by one to Smalls, who would leap through the hoop of fire and catch the sticks with his tongue in a grand and sparkling display.

Finally, Lord Jest would spray water from his trunk in a perfect circle, dousing the flames in the hoop of fire. Only then would Claude step into the ring. He'd lift his top hat—

and out would leap Tilda, doing a flip–double axel–flip routine before landing gracefully on all fours. It was a finale more complex and gasp-inducing than any the Most Magnificent Traveling Circus had ever attempted. "It's going to knock Ames's socks off," Claude whispered to himself.

And it probably would, if what was supposed to happen happened. But right now, it didn't. Not even close.

There were two things that went right: Susan leapt off Juliet's back at just the right time, and Lord Jest sprayed water from his trunk in a flawless circle, dousing the hoop. But everything else went awry.

Wombat teetered on the tightrope, plummeting to the ground after only two steps. Meanwhile, instead of leaping onto all fours atop the beach ball, Rigby flopped helplessly onto his stomach, and Smalls yelped out in pain as the hoop singed his paws, letting every one of the fire sticks crash to the ground. Finally, when Claude removed his top hat, Tilda tripped instead of leapt—tumbling to the ground without a single flip or axel.

It was, in a word, disastrous.

For a split second, everything was silent. Then, like a volcano, Claude erupted. "Worthless! I need *stars* for tomorrow. And what do I have? A wombat that can't use his claws. A rabbit that can't hop. A dog that can't balance." He stepped toward Smalls, swinging Wilson at his side. "And a sun bear with a USELESS TONGUE!"

Trembling, Smalls backed away, bumping into the edge of the ring. Claude stepped closer, raising the curved stick above his head. Smalls closed his eyes, bracing himself for the hit. *I'm in my oak tree,* he told himself. *I'm eating bucketfuls of honey.* But it didn't help. He could feel every one of his muscles quivering in fear.

"Looks like we Lifers are safe this time," Smalls heard Lord Jest jeer. "Master's got himself a brand-new punching bag."

"I think it's time you have a little run-in with Wilson, bear," Claude hissed. Suddenly, the stick was knifing through the air, lower, lower, lower—

"Wait!" Bertie's voice echoed through the tent. "I . . . I think I know why Smalls isn't catching the fire sticks."

"What did you say, boy?" Claude whipped around to face Bertie. Smalls blew out a sigh of relief as the stick dropped to his side.

"I think I can help," Bertie said quickly. Claude raised his bushy white eyebrows. "Let me work with Smalls, Uncle." A few feet away, Bertie could see Susan watching him. He straightened up to his full height, pushing his baseball cap off his forehead.

"Me too." Susan came over and stood next to Bertie, flashing him a tiny smile. "I can help Bertie."

Claude gnawed on a fingernail as he looked back and forth from Bertie to Susan. Bertie held his breath, hoping Susan couldn't hear the way his heart was hammering against his ribs.

"Fine." Claude spit the nail out at Bertie. "From now on, you two are in charge of the bear." He turned to Lloyd and Loyd. "And you two are in charge of the others." He nodded to himself, looking pleased. "And I," he muttered, "will be in charge of a nice, big jug of hot cocoa."

Clearing his throat, he waved for them to get started. "What are you waiting for? There's an important show tomorrow night, and I'm expecting it to be perfect." He looked at Bertie. "*All* of it."

Chapter Twenty-four

Bear Boy

Susan looked at Bertie. His mouth was set in a deter-mined line, but when he reached up to push a wisp of red hair out of his eyes, she saw how clammy his hands were. "It looks like we have a job to do," he said.

"So what's your idea?" Susan asked. She pinched his shoulder. "You *do* have an idea, right?"

Bertie laughed. "I have a theory," he told her. "I don't think Smalls is lifting his legs high enough when he jumps, which is why he keeps getting burned by the hoop. If he makes it through the hoop without getting burned, he'll have a much better shot at catching the fire sticks."

Susan nodded. "Makes sense."

Bertie glanced over his shoulder to where Lloyd and Loyd were trying unsuccessfully to teach Wombat to walk on the tightrope. Loyd threw up his hands in exasperation.

"Balance, you stupid wombat!"

"The problem is," Bertie said, "how do you explain that to a bear?"

Susan looked over at the bear. He was pressed up against the back of the ring, watching them cautiously. "Hi," she said softly.

"His name is Smalls," Bertie told her.

Susan took a step toward him. "Hi, Smalls," she said. Smalls cocked his furry head, watching her. His eyes were attentive, serious, but most of all scared. It made her want to fling her arms around him and hug him tight. The impulse took her by surprise. It had been six months since she'd hugged anyone at all.

She moved closer, slowly lifting her hand to pet him. Instantly, Smalls tensed, his eyes following her every movement. *He's paying attention,* she realized. It made her think of something her mom used to say. "Artists don't watch, Susan. They *see*."

"He sees," she said.

Bertie looked over at her curiously. "He has fine eyesight," he agreed. "As far as I can tell."

She shook her head. "It's more than that." And it gave her an idea. "I'll be right back."

"Where—?" Bertie began, but Susan had already disappeared backstage.

Bertie looked over at Smalls. He was cowering at the edge of the ring, looking terrified. Slowly, Bertie took a step toward him. "I'm not going to hurt you," he said soothingly. Smalls cocked his head, watching him, and Bertie hoped that in some way, he recognized the reassurance in his tone. "I'm not Claude," he went on, making his voice as unlike Claude's as possible. He took another step toward Smalls, fiddling with the slice of plum nestled at the bottom of his pocket.

His lunch that day had been a single scoop of dry oats, like usual. As he'd choked down the rock-solid bits, trying to ignore the way they cracked against his teeth and lodged themselves in his throat, he'd watched Claude devour a thick slice of doughy, cheesy pizza. With every bite Claude took, the pizza's hot cheese had stretched and pulled and snapped, its creamy tomato sauce dribbling down his chin. And the whole time, waiting for Claude on his plate, was a juicy purple plum. The plum had seemed to stare at Bertie as he finished his oats. *Think how delicious I'd taste,* it seemed to taunt. *Think how good I'd feel in your stomach.*

When Claude had started slicing the plum, its sweet, syrupy smell filling the air, Bertie hadn't been able to take it anymore. He *had* to have a slice. "Uncle," he'd said slowly, unable to draw his eyes away from the plum. "I think I hear the hot cocoa truck outside." Once a month, a special motorcar delivered Claude's hot cocoa to wherever the circus was performing that week, and Claude made sure he never missed it.

"You do? But they just came last week!" When Claude rushed outside to search for the truck, Bertie quickly plucked a large slice of plum off his plate, dropping it into his pocket.

All day long, Bertie had saved that plum. He'd been planning to eat it after dinner, to rid the chalky taste of oats from his mouth. But now, as Bertie stood in the ring, looking at Smalls's soot-covered muzzle and scorched fur, he knew he couldn't keep the fruit for himself. In one more step, Bertie was standing next to Smalls. "Here," he said, holding the plum out on his palm. He angled his back so neither of the Lloyds could see him. "It's for you."

Pressed up against the barrier of the ring, Smalls stared at the slice of plum in Bertie's hand. His breakfast that morning had been another serving of crusty, congealed slop, and although he'd forced it down, his stomach was already rumbling for something more. He looked up at Bertie.

"Go on," Bertie urged. "Take it."

So Smalls did. He stretched his long tongue out, snatching up the plum. Instantly, the juice exploded in his mouth, as cool and sweet as Smalls was hot and achy. He let out a sigh of pleasure as it slid down his throat, pooling softly in his stomach.

Bertie smiled as he watched Smalls eat. His eyes were closed and for a second, he looked almost relaxed. Gently, Bertie reached out and scratched Smalls under his chin. Smalls let out a pleased grunt, looking up at Bertie with wide, dark eyes. "It's going to be okay," Bertie whispered. "I'm watching out for you now."

If only he could understand me, Bertie thought. But Smalls was a bear. He didn't speak the language of boy.

Smalls leaned into Bertie's hand. *Thank you,* he wanted to say. But Bertie was a boy. He didn't speak the language of bear. So instead Smalls stretched out his tongue and gave Bertie's hand a big, wet lick.

"You have a good way with him." Bertie jumped a little at the sound of Susan's voice. He'd been so focused on Smalls that he hadn't heard her come up behind him. He glanced over his shoulder to find her smiling at him. "It's almost like you two were talking to each other." She laughed. "Which obviously isn't possible. *Unless . . .*" She studied him thoughtfully. "*Unless* you were a bear in another life!" She nudged him playfully in the side. "Is that it, Bear Boy?"

Bertie broke into a grin. *Bear Boy.* He liked the sound of that. With his bear at his side, he could gallop across fields and leap up mountains in a single bound. He gave Smalls another scratch under the chin. Now, that was a hero he'd like to be. He looked over at Susan. "I *have* been told I growl in my sleep . . ." he said. He couldn't help but beam a little when she laughed. "So tell me: what's your idea for this bear?"

Chapter Twenty-five

A Hug

Susan led Bertie over to the flaming hoop. "I filled the animals' water bucket up backstage," she said, tapping the bucket with her foot. "Will you help me lift it so we can put the fire out?"

"What does this have to do with your idea?" Bertie asked as they doused the flames with water.

"Here's what I'm thinking." Susan paced around the hoop as she talked. "Smalls seems really perceptive. He wasn't just watching us before. He was *seeing* us. He was paying attention. So it made me wonder. What if I actually *demonstrate* how he's supposed to jump? Maybe it will help him understand."

Bertie stared at her for a second. "That's brilliant," he said slowly.

Susan felt a blush creep onto her cheeks, and she quickly willed it away. Since when did she *blush*? "I don't know about that," she said. "But I think it's a worth a shot." Pushing a strand of blond hair out of her eyes, she got down on all fours.

She heard Bertie let out a surprised chuckle above her. "You weren't kidding around about demonstrating."

"Of course not," Susan replied in her most nasal Claude voice. "There's no *kidding around* at the circus!"

Bertie burst out laughing. He had a nice laugh, Susan decided. The kind that made you want to join in. "Sorry," he gasped. "You just look funny like that."

Susan gave her hair an indignant toss. "Well, get ready to laugh even harder, Bear Boy. Because I'm about to jump through that hoop." She whistled loudly, drawing Smalls's attention to her. "Watch this, Smalls!"

Moving forward on all fours, she neared the hoop. When she was just a few inches away, she let out her best bear-like grunt and—pretending her arms were front paws—she lifted them into the air. Tucking them close to her body, she pushed off the ground with her toes. Then she dove through the hoop like a bear.

As she soared through the air, the rest of the world seemed to fall away and for a second she was back in her ballet class at home, leaping to the crescendo of a violin. But as she landed gracefully on the other side of the hoop, reality returned with a bang, and once again she was at the circus, miles and miles away from home. She turned around to find Bertie gaping at her.

"How did you *do* that?" he exclaimed. In the back of the ring, she could see Lloyd and Loyd watching too, both their jaws hanging open.

Susan shrugged nonchalantly, but she couldn't help but feel a flicker of pride. "I was a ballet dancer before I was an acrobat," she told him. "In a way, it's just like leaping." She walked over to Smalls. "The real question is if *he* saw that." She gave Smalls a pat on the head. "So did you, boy? Did you see the way I tucked my 'paws' to my chest when I jumped?"

Smalls stretched out his tongue, giving her a lick on the hand.

"I think that means yes," Bertie translated. "But just to be safe, you should probably demonstrate a few more times." He grinned at her. "Back on your paws, Bear Girl."

Several hours later, Bertie tossed a fire stick into the air for the umpteenth time, watching as it spun upward. Ever since Susan had finished demonstrating for Smalls, they'd been practicing with him nonstop, throwing fire stick after fire stick as he leapt through the flaming hoop. And all that time, they'd been talking too, about anything and everything: her parents, his vanished memories, their favorite places the circus had traveled to. "So where do you paint?" Bertie asked Susan, keeping his voice down so Lloyd and Loyd couldn't hear. She'd just finished telling him about her paint set, how she wasn't sure if she could have made it through these past six months without it.

"Anywhere I can." She said it so fiercely he had to smile. "When I find scraps of paper—which is rare—I'll paint in my sleeping compartment. But most of the time I sneak off the circus grounds and find places to paint outside." Her whole face lit up when she talked about painting, and Bertie couldn't draw his eyes away from her as he threw several more fire sticks for Smalls. "I've found my best place yet at this venue," Susan went on. "A cave at the foot of the woods. It's amazing, Bertie. When I'm there, it's like . . . I have a place all my own."

Bertie threw another fire stick into the air. "I don't even remember what that feels like," he said quietly. He thought of his sleeping cubby, where Claude was constantly barging in. Even that tiny, minuscule place wasn't his own.

"You should sneak away to my cave before we move on to the next venue," Susan told him. She shot him a mischievous look. "I swear you won't find a single drop of cocoa there."

Bertie laughed. "Sounds like my kind of place." He tossed up the last fire stick, and Smalls caught it easily, like he had all the others.

Susan clapped for him. "He's really getting it."

"Your crazy demonstration actually worked," Bertie replied, shaking his head in awe.

Susan raised her eyebrows at him. "Never doubt me, Bear Boy."

Bertie laughed as he held his hand out for Smalls. Smalls trotted over, carefully dropping the sticks into his palm, flames pointing outward.

"One more time?" Susan asked.

Bertie nodded. "Let's see what this bear can do."

Bertie held up the flickering fire sticks, and Smalls crouched in front of the hoop, his ears bent low. "One," Susan counted. "Two. Go!" She clapped, and Smalls sprang into the air, tucking his legs tightly beneath him. As he landed easily on the other side of the hoop, not a single flame biting at his fur, Bertie began to throw the fire sticks.

Smalls waited until the first fire stick was right in front of him, then he flicked out his tongue, catching the non-lit end. "One," Susan cheered.

Smalls caught another one, then another. Soon there was only one fire stick left, hurtling toward him. Susan reached out and squeezed Bertie's arm. "Come on, Smalls," she murmured. Smalls leaned forward. With an effortless swipe of his tongue, he caught the final stick. He lifted his head proudly, six flames sparkling above him.

"Yes!" Susan shouted. She threw her arms around Bertie, hugging him tight.

Bertie's breath caught in his throat. Susan was hugging him. Her hair brushed against his shoulder, and he could smell the faintest scent of freshness—like grass and trees—lingering on it. Then just as quickly, she pulled away.

"I-I'm sorry," she stammered. Her face was flushed and her eyes flitted around the ring, refusing to meet his. "I shouldn't have . . . I just got caught up in . . ." She trailed off, tugging nervously at a strand of hair.

"No, it's fine," Bertie said quickly. He could feel his face growing hot, like his freckles had caught on fire. "I didn't . . . I mean . . ."

"I should go get water to put out the hoop," Susan said quickly.

"I should get the fire sticks from Smalls," Bertie added. Turning away, they both hurried in opposite directions.

"You were great," Bertie told Smalls, taking the fire sticks from him. As he blew them out, he couldn't help but peek over at Susan. She was dragging a full bucket of water over to the flaming hoop, her cheeks still flushed. Bertie pushed his baseball cap off his forehead. He thought about the way her arms had tightened around his neck, how her hair had brushed against his shoulder. It should have felt strange to him, alien, but instead it had just felt easy.

"Here," he said, going over to the hoop. "I'll help you."

They had just poured the water over the flames when one of the Lloyds called out for Bertie. "Time for dinner, boy! Chain up the bear." Bertie looked over his shoulder to see the Lloyds chaining up the rest of the animals. "We're leaving 'em in here while we eat," Lloyd added, tossing Bertie a chain. It clanged against his leg as he caught it.

"Sorry, Smalls," Bertie said, clipping the chain around the bear's paws as loosely as he could.

"Sorry?" Lloyd snorted. He elbowed his twin in the side. "The boy just *apologized* to the bear, Loyd."

Loyd threw his head back, laughing. "That bear can't understand you, stupid boy. And even if he could, you know what your uncle taught us. Animals don't have feelings!"

Chapter Twenty-six

In Your Dreams

Smalls had never been so tired in his life. He collapsed on the ground in the ring, resting his head on his paws. He was too tired to move. He was too tired to play. He was even too tired to make a list. *I think I'll take a little nap,* he decided. His eyes had just drifted shut when a sound from the front of the ring stirred him awake. Groggily, he opened his eyes.

Buck was crouched down in front of Tilda, nudging her with his nose. "You. Me. That private corner over there," he was saying. "How about it, sweet thing?"

"Absolutely not!" Wombat cut in. He stepped bravely in front of Buck, his snout held high, but Buck easily kicked him away.

"Believe me, bunny buns," Buck said to Tilda. "You don't know what you're missing. It's time you dated a *real* animal."

"With a *real* name." Hamlet snickered.

"My friends call me Fred!" Wombat bellowed, stomping his paw against the ground.

Ignoring Wombat, Buck tickled Tilda with his black and white tail. "Come on, bunny love," he flirted. "We're perfect for each other."

"Perfect for each other?" Wombat sputtered. "Your paw is bigger than her head!" He pushed his way back in front of Buck, but Buck just swatted him away again, sending him skidding across the ring.

"You . . . you brute!" Wombat yelled as he landed on his head.

Smalls leapt to his feet. Who did Buck think he was? He might be a zebra, but Smalls was a bear! And as far as he was concerned, claws trumped stripes any day of the week.

"Brute?" Hamlet laughed as Smalls stormed over to Buck. "Is that even a real word?"

"It's a real word," Juliet confirmed. She eyed Wombat disdainfully. "Though the verdict's still out on whether he's a real animal."

"For the last time," Wombat said, pulling himself back up. "I am a hairy-nosed—"

"May!" Juliet gasped.

"Not a hairy-nosed *May*," Wombat shouted in exasperation.

"A hairy-nosed . . ." But as Juliet ran to May, he suddenly fell silent. "Oh," he said shakily.

May the monkey had collapsed on the floor.

Smalls forgot about everything—Buck, Tilda, even Wombat—as he raced to Juliet's side. Within seconds, the rest of the animals had joined them.

May's eyes were closed, her breathing labored. "May?" Juliet said. When May didn't answer, Juliet prodded her with her nose. But still she didn't stir.

"Do you know what's wrong with her?" Smalls asked.

Juliet gently licked May's face, but May's eyes didn't open.

"What's wrong with her is this place!" Juliet exploded. "She's too old for this, too frail." She nudged May again as Hamlet and Buck paced in circles around her. Wombat and Tilda huddled by May's feet, with Rigby behind them. Only Lord Jest stood off to the corner, peering at May out of the corners of his eyes. "Wake up, May," Juliet begged. "Please."

As she licked May's fur, Smalls went over to the animals' water bucket, which Susan had filled up to the top. He grabbed the handle in his teeth, dragging the bucket over to May.

Juliet looked up, her yellow eyes flashing. "You really need a drink right now?" she snapped.

"No. But she might." With a grunt, Smalls shoved the bucket onto its side. Water poured over May, darkening her fur.

"Are you crazy?" Juliet yelled. She drew back her lip, revealing a gleaming white fang.

"Jul." Hamlet hit his sister with his tail. "Look."

On the ground, May's eyes were fluttering. "Juliet?" she whispered.

"May!" Juliet crouched by her side. "Are you all right?"

"Thirsty," May croaked. Gently, Juliet nudged May's head toward the pool of water that had gathered next to her. "Ah," May sighed as she lapped it up. "Better." She curled up against Juliet, who blanketed her with her thick, silky tail.

"Do you need anything else?" Juliet asked her quietly.

"I do." May drew in a long, raspy breath. "I need . . ." She paused, and the animals all leaned in close to hear her. "Bananas!" she finished with a weak smile.

As the rest of the animals burst out laughing, Juliet looked up at Smalls. "Thanks," she said. Then she turned briskly back to May. "Well, you better go back to sleep then," she teased. "Because the only place you're finding bananas is in your dreams."

Chapter Twenty-seven
Holy Horseshoe

Smalls was dreaming of honey. He was on a boat, crossing the ocean, but instead of water, the ocean was made of thick, gooey waves of honey.

He was just about to scoop up a pawful when a noise—a moan—suddenly shook him awake. He opened his eyes, a

thin line of sunlight streaming in at him from the caravan window. He was in a cage instead of a boat, not a drop of honey in sight. And every inch of his body—his head, his paws, his back, even his *claws*—was aching.

"Ooooo."

At the sound of the moan, Smalls pulled himself to his feet, ignoring the throbbing in his right paw. The sound was coming from May's cage.

"May?" Smalls whispered. But she just let out another moan. The sound wiggled its way into him, making him feel itchy in his own fur. He touched his ear, wishing desperately for a four-leaf clover. But of course, there was nothing there.

Pressing his muzzle against the bars of his cage, he looked out at May. Her legs were twitching, her stomach was heaving, and there was a strange red bump on her tail. It was the wound from falling off her unicycle, he realized. Overnight it had grown puffy and inflamed. Smalls didn't know a lot about cuts, but he did know they weren't supposed to look like that.

"What's she doing?" Juliet's voice made Smalls jump. He looked over to see her standing in her cage, swishing her tail in nervous circles. "I can't see her from over here!"

"She's asleep," Smalls said. "But . . . she doesn't look

good." He watched as May took a slow, wheezing breath. "I think it's her cut."

Juliet shook her head. "You can go back to sleep now," she said sharply. She kept her voice low, and in the cages around them, the other animals slept peacefully on. "I'll stay up with her."

Smalls ignored her. Stifling a yawn, he sat down, keeping his eyes on May. He could hear Juliet's tail swishing back and forth, back and forth in her cage. As May let out another moan, he shook his head. "Holy horseshoe," he said softly.

"Holy *what*?" Juliet asked.

"Horseshoe," Smalls sniffed.

Juliet studied him curiously. "Are you sure you don't mean holy mackerel? Or holy moly?"

Smalls rubbed at the yellow horseshoe on his chest. "Holy horseshoe," he repeated firmly.

Juliet cocked her head. "Holy horseshoe," she tried out. She looked almost amused, but before she could say anything else, the door to the caravan swung open. Lloyd and Loyd stomped in, followed by Bertie. As Bertie headed through the caravan with the animals' trays of slop, his eyes fell on May.

He let out a gasp, stopping short. "Look at May!" he told the Lloyds.

The twins clomped over to May's cage, peering inside. "That monkey does not look good," Lloyd said.

The twins exchanged a befuddled look.

"Boss left us in charge of the morning rounds," Lloyd said nervously.

"He told us not to bother him no matter *what*," Loyd agreed anxiously.

Smalls watched as Bertie crouched next to May's cage, reaching through the bars to pet her. "We need a vet," he said, his voice tight. "Now."

"Ha!" Loyd scoffed. "Vets are expensive, boy."

"And that monkey's worth nothing at this point," Lloyd chimed in. "Nada. Zip. Zero." He smiled a little, looking proud of his vocabulary.

"We're just going to have to fix this on our own," Loyd said.

Side by side, the twins began to pace through the caravan. "Maybe we can dump her in the woods," Loyd suggested.

Smalls looked over at them sharply. *Dump her?*

Across the way, Juliet sucked in a breath. All around him, Smalls could hear the other animals waking—stirring and stretching in their cages—but he kept his eyes trained on the Lloyds, watching as they paced along the length of the caravan. "That's genius," Lloyd replied excitedly.

"Then Boss would never have to pay another vet bill for her again!"

"Um, Lloyd?" Bertie ventured. "Loyd?"

"Boss *was* just saying how useless the monkey is these days," Loyd went on, ignoring Bertie. "I bet he'd be thrilled if we tossed her in the woods."

Smalls growled under his breath. *Tossed her?*

"Lloyd?" Bertie tried again. "Loyd?"

"We'd have to make sure no one saw us, of course," Lloyd pointed out.

"Or heard us," Loyd added.

"LLOYDS!"

Both Lloyds sighed impatiently. "What is it, boy?"

"What about the monkey sanctuary?" Bertie asked hurriedly. "The one we passed on the drive here? What if we brought her there?"

"Smalls?" Rigby's bark drifted over from his cage, drawing Smalls's attention away from the humans. "What's going on?"

"May's sick," Smalls told him softly.

"Sick?" Tilda squeaked in horror. Smalls could hear her shaking out her fur, the first step in her morning grooming process.

Lloyd let out a loud laugh before the animals could say

anything else. "Why would we want to take her all the way to a sanctuary, boy, when the woods are right here?"

"Because . . ." Bertie paused, and from the look on his face, Smalls could tell he was thinking hard. "Because I bet we'd get written up in the newspaper for it! I can see the headline now," he continued hastily. "The Most Magnificent Traveling Circus Donates Monkey to Sanctuary!" He smiled persuasively up at Lloyd and Loyd. "Just think how grateful Claude would be if you got the circus written up in the newspaper."

"Claude does love newspapers," Lloyd said thoughtfully.

"And he loves being in them even more," Loyd added eagerly.

The twins looked at each other. "Maybe we'll get a promotion," Lloyd whispered to Loyd.

"Maybe we'll get a raise," Loyd whispered to Lloyd.

They both nodded. "Get the monkey, boy," Lloyd ordered, tossing Bertie a ring of keys. "We're going to the sanctuary."

Chapter Twenty-eight

What's Black and White and Red All Over?

L oyd pulled the old black motorcar into a winding dirt driveway. WELCOME TO RAINTREE SANCTUARY, the sign at the end of the driveway read. THE HOME OF YOUR MONKEY'S DREAMS!

"Dreams?" Lloyd scoffed from the passenger seat. "Monkeys don't dream."

"That would be like saying animals understand *English*," Loyd chimed in with a laugh.

In the backseat of the car, Bertie swallowed back a groan. Next to him, inside a cardboard box that had CARA'S COCOA, THE BEST COCOA IN THE WORLD! printed on the side, was May. She was still asleep, breathing heavily. The cut on her tail had grown more swollen, the edges a bright, blistering red, and every so often, a deep shiver racked through her. Bertie put his hand on her head, stroking her whiskers as the motorcar jolted to a stop with a sputter of smoke.

"This better be quick," Loyd said as he climbed out of the car. "We don't want to keep Boss waiting."

Carefully, Bertie picked up the box, trying not to jostle May as he lifted it out of the car. Lloyd honked the car's horn several times, and a minute later, a large woman waddled out of Raintree. "Hello!" she sang out. "Welcome to Raintree! The Home of Your Monkey's Dreams! Here at Raintree, we make sure each of our monkeys gets the utmost in care! They have acres to swing through! Trees to sleep in! Shelter for when it's cold! And of course, unlimited bananas to eat!"

Inside the cardboard box, May shifted. She opened one eye a crack. "Bananas?" she croaked.

"Great, great," Loyd said, waving dismissively. "Here." He grabbed the box out of Bertie's arms, shoving it at the woman. "We have a monkey for you." He proudly squared his shoulders. "When you talk to the newspaper, you can thank Loyd and Lloyd of the Most Magnificent Traveling Circus."

The woman's eyes widened as she looked down at the moaning, shivering monkey. "Oh dear," she said.

"Bananas?" May wheezed.

"What's her name?" the woman asked.

Loyd shrugged. "June? August? Something like that."

"May," Bertie jumped in, clenching his fists at his sides. "Her name's May."

The woman smiled brightly. "What a beautiful name. Here at Raintree, we like our monkeys to have names that exemplify their personalities—"

"Yeah, yeah," Loyd cut in. "Now, when the newspaper calls, don't forget to tell them it was Loyd and Lloyd who brought the monkey. That's Loyd with one *L* and Lloyd with two *L*'s." He leaned forward, lowering his voice. "But make sure you say Loyd with one *L* first."

The woman blinked, looking confused. "Newspaper?"

Bertie tensed. He had a feeling they better get out of there before the Lloyds realized he'd made up the newspaper article. "Claude's waiting for us," he said abruptly. "We don't want to be late for practice."

Loyd flinched, and it hit Bertie suddenly that even though the Lloyds were three times his size and had the kind of muscles that bulged right out of their shirts, they were just as scared of Claude as he was. "Well, then, stop wasting time, boy," Loyd said. He grabbed Bertie's arm, yanking him back into the car.

As they sped out of the driveway, their tires screeching, Bertie twisted around just in time to see the woman pull open Raintree's gate, revealing a huge greenhouse filled with trees—bananas dangling from every one. Bertie smiled to himself as he turned around again. May wasn't going to miss the circus one bit.

While May got settled in at the home of her dreams, Juliet was back at the circus along with the other animals, turning in nervous circles inside the ring. "She's gone," she said miserably. "I can't believe May's really gone."

Hamlet let out a soft growl. "I'm sorry, Jul."

"Whatcha moaning on about?" Lord Jest tossed his trunk. "She got sent to a sanctuary! That's like monkey heaven! She shoulda smashed her tail up years ago."

"Lord Jest!" Juliet scolded. "You didn't hear her earlier. She was . . . I thought . . ." Tears welled in her eyes and she quickly looked down at the ground.

"Come on, Juliet," Lord Jest scoffed. "Whadya think woulda happened if May hadn't left? She woulda brought us all down tonight with her terrible performance, and all us Lifers woulda suffered! You should be *grateful* she's gone."

"How can you say that?" The question flew out of Smalls's mouth before he could stop it.

Every muscle in Lord Jest's massive body tensed. "'Scuse me?" he said slowly. "What didya say to me?"

Taking a deep breath, Smalls walked over to the elephant.

"I *said*, how can you say something like that? May was your friend!"

Lord Jest looked right at Smalls, narrowing his eyes. "There's no such thing as friends in the circus, buddy bear. Here, ya just do what ya gotta to survive."

Smalls shook his head. "That isn't right," he said softly.

"I've been here a whole lot longer than you," Lord Jest replied with a shrug of his trunk. "I've seen animals come, I've seen animals die. Ya learn not to get attached. When ya care is when ya get in trouble."

"Except when you care about me," Buck said, sidling up to Tilda. He gave her a pouty face. "Hi, my pretty puff. How about you console this grieving zebra when we get to practice?"

"I—" Tilda began, but Wombat cut her off.

"She will do nothing of the sort!" he snapped. But once again, Buck just ignored him.

"I've got a joke for you, honey bunny," he said, ruffling his mane. "What's black and white and red all over?"

"A sunburned penguin?" Tilda squeaked.

"No." Buck winked at her as he lowered his voice. "This zebra when you make him blush."

"Stop it!" Wombat hollered. "Don't you understand? She. Hates. STRIPES!"

"Wombat!" Tilda gasped. "Calm down!"

But Wombat didn't seem to hear her. "She. Likes. WOM-BATS!"

Buck brayed in amusement. "We'll see about that, guinea pig."

Wombat's ears flattened against his head. "I," he said through gritted teeth, "am a HAIRY-NOSED—"

Before he could finish, the door to the caravan swung open. "You brought the monkey to a *sanctuary*?" Claude bellowed as he stormed inside. Lloyd and Loyd followed, with chains piled high in their arms.

"It's going to make the circus famous," Lloyd said knowingly.

"We'll be written up in the newspaper," Loyd said resolutely.

Claude stopped short, looking from Loyd to Lloyd and back again. He was wearing an outfit of all orange, a jug of cocoa clutched in his hands. "I put you two in charge for *one* morning so I can attend to some business, and this is what happens?" He paused, gulping back some cocoa. "You're just lucky that old monkey was useless to me!" With another pause, he drained the rest of the jug. "Now stop wasting time! We only have nine hours before Ames—*ahem*, I mean the audience arrives tonight." With that, he stalked out of the caravan, muttering to himself about a cocoa refill.

Lloyd looked at Loyd.

Loyd looked at Lloyd.

"He'll change his mind when he sees the newspaper article," Loyd said.

Lloyd nodded his agreement. "Then we'll get raises for sure."

Chapter Twenty-nine

Let the Show Begin

The day passed in a whirlwind of practice. Hour after hour the animals worked on their acts, and slowly but surely the finale came together. Wombat made it all the way across the tightrope. Rigby jumped up on the beach ball and didn't fall right back down. Tilda nailed her flip–double axel– flip combo with a thrilled squeak. And Smalls leapt through the flaming hoop and caught six fire sticks in a row without a single burn or yelp.

With an hour to showtime, Claude looked almost happy, a tight smile spreading across his lips. "Bajumba," he whis- pered. "Ames is going to like what he sees." With a stroke of his beard, he cleared his throat. "Lloyd," he barked.

"Yes, Boss?" Loyd said.

"Yes, Boss?" Lloyd added.

"Bring the animals backstage." He turned to Bertie. "You

clean up their equipment. And you." His gaze moved to Susan. "What are you waiting for? Go get your rope ready!"

Susan nodded. "Of course, Master Magnificence," she said, her voice extra bright. But as she passed by Bertie, she crossed her eyes at him when Claude wasn't looking.

An hour later, Smalls was sitting backstage, rubbing anxiously at the yellow horseshoe on his chest as he waited for the circus to begin. He felt like electricity was zipping through him, prickling at his paws and buzzing in his ears. All day long, he'd kept looking around, hoping to spot a four-leaf clover poking out of the dusty ground or peeking up through a crack in the Big Top. But nothing green seemed to grow here. Not grass, not trees, not flowers, and certainly not clovers.

"Step three, done," Tilda murmured nearby. She was ticking off each step as she made her way through her sixteen-step grooming process. "Skip step four," she muttered angrily. "Since I no longer have my red silk bow."

Next to her, Wombat was whispering to himself in French and Rigby was debating the tent's exact shade of red. "Redwood," he said. "No, rose! No." His tail thumped excitedly against the ground. "Ruby! Definitely ruby."

Smalls glanced around, trying to distract himself. In the back of the tent, the acrobats and tumblers were stretching and warming up, touching their toes and jogging in place and kicking their legs above their heads. Susan was carefully unwrapping strips of gauze from around her hands, a focused expression on her face. The clowns were scattered about, adjusting their wigs and honking each other's noses and singing scales to prepare their voices. Nearby, the horn player was shining his horn and Claude was shining his top hat and even Buck was shining his hooves with his tail. The lions were busy too, Hamlet fluffing out his mane and Juliet buffing her fur. It seemed like everyone had something to do except for him.

Nosing the curtain back, Smalls peered into the ring. It was the smell that hit him first: swirls of cinnamon and sugar and dough, so thick and fragrant he could almost see them. The ring had a red velvet floor, and just minutes earlier, Smalls had watched Loyd and Lloyd run out with a bucket of red paint to fill in spots that had worn thin since the last show. But looking at it now, you'd never know. Under the sparkling circus lights, the floor looked plush and bright. Curved along the outside of the ring were rows of silver benches. People were filing into them, holding pillowy donuts and fizzing sodas and soft puffs of spun sugar. A boy with a headful of brown curls gripped a twisty bun stuffed with cinnamon, making Smalls's mouth water.

Suddenly, the lights in the tent dimmed. "Let the show begin," Smalls heard Claude murmur as the audience jostled to take their seats. Claude clapped briskly. "You're up, Larry."

A clown wearing oversized polka-dot pants held up by thick green suspenders straightened out his orange wig. His face was painted white, and a squeaky red ball was perched on his nose. He paused behind the curtain, dropping twelve juggling balls into his large pockets. Out in the ring, the lights went out completely, an oily darkness sweeping over everything. Squaring his shoulders, Larry the Clown walked out to perform.

Alone in the center of the ring, he began to juggle. As he tossed the balls into the air, they lit up, one by one, until they were glowing like a dozen moons. Their shadows flitted across the tent's ceiling, bending and waving and twisting, never still. It made Smalls think of nighttime at Mumford's, how the inky sky would coil into shapes behind the stars, like the darkness was telling a story.

The balls winked and flashed as they began to fall, and then with a *pop*, they each flickered out, darkening the ring once again. For a second, everything was silent. Even the audience seemed to hold their collective breaths. Then, all at once, the horn blasted and the tent brightened, pinpricks of light raining down on the ring.

The clown was gone, and in his place was Claude, the ringmaster, resplendent in an outfit of pure gold: shiny gold shoes, gold pants made of brushed velvet, a tight gold vest with gold buttons that looked ready to pop, and a gold top-coat with coattails that flapped behind him. On his head was a gold top hat, with a band of shimmering gold gems along the brim.

"Welcome to the Most Magnificent Traveling Circus!" Claude announced. His voice was different than usual, lighter and less nasal, like it was tap-dancing through the air. It made him sound like someone else entirely. "Our acts are sure to delight and thrill you, to entertain and amuse you, to excite and inspire you. So sit back, relax, and most of all, enjoy the show!" With a tip of his gold top hat, Claude disappeared into the fold of the curtain, slipping backstage.

"Tumblers," he hissed as the horn blasted through the ring. His voice was his own again, sharp and nasal. "You're up."

Dressed in matching tie-dyed bodysuits, the Nilling cousins burst into the tent, diving into a synchronized routine. "Lloyd, get the elephant ready," Claude commanded. "And then Loyd, the lions. They're up next!"

As the Lifers and performers cycled in and out of the tent, Smalls could hear Rigby, Tilda, and Wombat whispering behind him. But he couldn't make himself focus on their words. He just kept thinking how soon *he* would be out there, hundreds of eyes pressing in on him from every side. Back at Mumford's, they used to play in front of crowds all the time, but this was different. This crowd wanted something. *Expected* something. This wasn't a game.

Smalls drew in a long breath. Practicing with Bertie earlier, swiping fire sticks out of the air like they were nothing but flies, he'd felt ready for this. But now, peeking through the curtain from backstage, watching Lord Jest shoot spirals of water out of his trunk and Buck lobby pins into the air with his nose, he wasn't so sure. His paws felt soft and wobbly, like they were made of jelly, and suddenly he couldn't remember if he had to jump two feet or three feet to clear the hoop. An awful list started to assemble in his head.

Things That Could Go Wrong

1. Every single strand of my fur could go up in flames.

2. I could slip and send every strand of Rigby's fur up in flames.

3. He could slip and send every bristly fur on Wombat up in flames.

4. We could all go up in flames. Except for Claude and his little friend, Wilson.

Smalls rubbed at the yellow horseshoe on his chest. At

least Claude had decided to save the Misfits' performance for the finale. *His final surprise,* he kept calling it. Which was fine by Smalls. One chance to go up in flames was more than enough.

"Five minutes!" Loyd grabbed Smalls by the scruff of his neck. "Get in line, Misfits. You're on next."

Chapter Thirty
A Finale to Remember

Out in the front of the Big Top, Bertie was pouring sodas, endless streams of sweet, bubbly syrup, each snatched away by eager hands before he could take even a single taste for himself. "I want a donut, Mother!" a girl demanded shrilly. She had wild brown curls and was wearing a yellow dress that had a poufy skirt, as if there were hundreds of juggling balls stuffed underneath. She dragged a small dollhouse behind her, eying the donut counter greedily.

"We'll get you one, Chrysanthemum," her mom promised. She had a pale face and nervous, watery eyes. "As soon as we get our soda. Just please don't shriek." She handed Bertie a coin. "Two colas," she ordered.

"Extra, extra syrupy," the yellow dress girl—Chrysanthemum, whatever kind of name *that* was—added snottily. "And fill it all the way to the top."

Bertie struggled not to roll his eyes as he poured the colas for the girl and her mom. A tiny bit fizzed onto his hand, and his stomach gurgled at the thought of sucking it up. But as the girl snatched the soda from him, it dripped off, sinking into the velvet floor.

She still wears diapers under her poufy dresses, Bertie decided. It was a game he liked to play with the worst kids: imagining up terrible facts about them. Just minutes ago, he'd decided that a screaming, red-faced boy was wearing socks filled to the top with cow manure.

Chrysanthemum moved on to the donut stand, and a small blond boy, maybe four or five, took her place. He was with his mom, who kept ruffling his hair, making it flop into his face. "Stop it, Mom," he groaned, but he was laughing as he said it, and he leaned against her leg, letting her support his weight.

Bertie stood still, waiting for the longing to hit. It always happened when he saw a boy laughing with his mom. Sometimes the longing squeezed him so tightly that the whole world seemed to spin, and he had to close his eyes until it passed. But today, Bertie found himself thinking about Susan instead and how good it had felt to laugh lately, that kind of deep-down laughter that made him feel like he was splitting at the seams. Bertie smiled absently as he handed the boy his cola.

"Thanks!" the boy chirped. He grabbed his mom's hand,

dragging her toward the tent. "Hurry, Mom," he pleaded. "I don't want to miss the finale."

Bertie glanced around. The concession stands had emptied out, and there wasn't a single person waiting in line for soda. He seized his chance, hurrying over to the curtain to peek into the ring. Claude didn't like him to watch the show. "Concession counters should be manned at all times," he always said. Bertie wasn't even supposed to break for the bathroom. But usually, when he was sure Claude was safely backstage, he would sneak a peek anyway. And after all his work with Smalls, there was no way he was missing tonight's finale.

Susan was in the ring, finishing up her performance on the rope. She'd threaded white ribbons through her hair, and they fluttered behind her like wings as she soared and spun and dipped. But this time as Bertie watched, he didn't see the ribbons, or the twirls, or the way her blond hair fanned out behind her, shimmering under the light. Instead, he saw her hands, raw and sore with blisters. It made him want to run into the ring and help her down from the rope, tell her she never had to spin or twirl or twist again.

As Susan performed her final rotation, the animals were lining up backstage. "This is it," Claude kept saying. He was pacing back and forth, stroking furiously at his beard. "I'm going to blow Ames Howard away with this finale," Smalls heard him whisper to himself. "And then he'll *have* to—"

"Now!" Loyd said, drowning out the rest of Claude's sentence. He shoved Smalls toward the opening in the curtain. Susan had just leapt off the rope and was curtsying to a standing ovation. As she disappeared backstage, Loyd kicked Smalls in the back, and suddenly he was flying through the curtain and out into the ring. Smalls blinked under the bright lights as the other animals spilled out around him. The horn blasted, once, twice, three times. Lord Jest swung his trunk majestically through the air. The finale had begun.

At first, everything went like clockwork. Lord Jest flung his hula hoops and Susan slid easily down his trunk and Hamlet and Juliet spun so fast they were almost a blur. Buck ran alongside them, juggling balls under his hooves and behind his tail, making the audience go wild.

Then came Wombat's turn. Looking terrified, Wombat took one step onto the rope. Then another, and another. Slowly, a look of confidence crept onto his face. He lifted his snout up, walking faster, his steps steady and sure. "I'm doing it, Tilda," he called out. "It turns out I'm quite the audacious wombat!"

Wombat had just made it past the middle of the rope when out of nowhere, his paw slipped. He let out a gasp as his legs splayed out beneath him, sending him belly-flopping onto the rope. "I can remedy this," he said as he bounced up and down on his stomach. "I'm audacious. I'm skillful. I'm—"

"Falling." Lord Jest laughed.

He was right. With one more bounce, Wombat slid off the rope, crashing to the ground with a resounding thud. At that moment, Rigby jumped onto his beach ball as planned. Instantly, it deflated beneath him. He too tumbled to the ground, landing with a yelp in a tangled pile of fur.

Smalls glanced wildly around. The Lifers were still performing, as if they hadn't even seen Rigby and Wombat fall. Lord Jest was bending a hula hoop into the shape of a poodle with his trunk, Hamlet and Juliet were zooming around the ring on their wheel, and Buck was juggling fifteen balls effortlessly through the air. As Wombat and Rigby pulled themselves back up, an image of Wilson, Claude's stick, flashed through Smalls's mind. *It's up to me now,* he realized.

Susan leapt gracefully off Juliet's back in the front of the ring. She turned the hoop of fire on and instantly it burst into flames. "Let's save this," she whispered.

"You read my mind," Smalls replied. Though of course, to Susan, it sounded like a long grunt.

Smalls took his place by the hoop. *One,* he counted silently. *Two. Go!* As he leapt into the air, tucking his legs beneath him, the ring seemed to melt away, until it was just him and the hoop. And suddenly he knew: he could do this. He soared through the air, clearing the hoop easily. A burst of pride rushed through him. He hoped that wherever Bertie was, he saw that.

Quickly, Smalls tilted his head up, preparing for the fire sticks. Behind him, he heard the telltale sizzle of Susan throwing the first one. He unfurled his long tongue, his fur prickling in anticipation. But as the fire stick arched into the air, the flames that usually flickered from its tip kept growing—and growing, and growing. Smalls heard Susan let out a gasp as the flames grew so large they engulfed the stick, until it wasn't so much a fire stick as a ball of fire.

Smalls couldn't tear his eyes away from the mass of flames as it began to hurtle downward. Closer and closer it drew, growing larger and stronger with every passing second. Smalls stood up tall, stretching out his tongue. He could do this. He *had* to do this. But then the ball of fire was right above him, and he could feel the heat pouring off it in waves. There was no stick left to catch on his tongue, only flames. And suddenly he could feel the way they would singe his tongue and scorch his fur, sending bolts of pain shooting through him. With a yelp, he leapt out of the way—just in time for the ball of fire to come crashing down in the front of the ring.

Sparks flew as it collided with the floor, the smell of burnt velvet rising into the air. The flames continued to grow, feeding on each other as they flickered left and right. Smalls jumped backward as a flame blazed by, nearly licking at his paws. "Watch out!" Susan yelled, pushing Smalls away from another patch of fire. As plumes of smoke rose around him, Smalls's heart clenched up in his chest.

The ring of the Big Top was officially on fire.

Chapter Thirty-one

How 'Bout the Elephant?

As the fire blazed in the front of the ring, the audience stumbled over each other to get to the exit. "Wait!" Claude yelled, bursting through the curtain from backstage. In his haste, he tripped over Rigby's deflated beach ball. Stumbling forward, he landed sprawled out on his oversized belly, a few feet away from the flames. His top hat slid off and out shot Tilda. She was slathered head to toe in mud, looking more like a bedraggled mouse than a majestic rabbit.

Hopping faster than Smalls had ever seen her move, Tilda hurried to the back of the ring, away from the flames, and immediately began licking the mud off her paws. Smalls, Wombat, and Rigby quickly joined her, huddling together as the flames rose ahead of them.

As Claude struggled to pull himself up from the ground, the distinct sound of popping came from underneath his wide girth. Finally, he managed to stand, but as he did, seven gold buttons scattered onto the ground. His vest sprang open, revealing a torn and stained undershirt beneath it. "Water!" Claude screamed as smoke rose around him. "Someone get me water!"

Backstage, Loyd tripped over Lloyd as they both dove for the animals' water bucket. Their legs tangled together and they both went plummeting to the ground, landing face-first in the bucket. "Get me out of here!" Loyd yelled through a mouthful of water. Their arms and legs flailed in unison as they both fought to get out of the bucket first.

"You almost drowned me!" Lloyd yelled as he finally sat up, water streaming down his face.

"You almost drowned *me*!" Loyd yelled back, water gurgling from his nose.

"Me!"

"Me!"

Suddenly Lloyd paused. "Was there something we were supposed to be doing?" he asked.

"I think there was," Loyd replied thoughtfully. "And I think it was this!" With a gleeful laugh, he shoved his brother's face back into the bucket of water.

Out in the ring, Lord Jest was dipping his trunk into his own bucket of water, sucking up every last drop.

"Water!" Claude yelled again. "Someone! Now!" His eyes landed on a man in a suit, who was running full speed toward the exit, pushing kids out of the way left and right. "Ames!" Claude called out. "Don't leave!" But the man in the suit ignored him, sprinting out of the tent.

Behind Claude, Lord Jest calmly lifted his trunk out of the bucket. Aiming it at the tallest flames, he shot out a powerful stream of water. "How 'bout that?" He beamed as the flames sputtered and died out, leaving nothing but a smoldering pile of ash behind. Sweeping his trunk through the front of the ring, Lord Jest shot water at every flame and spark and sizzle. Within seconds, he'd put the entire fire out before it could spread outside the ring.

The tent fell suddenly and completely still. Screams faded and footsteps halted and every eye in the tent turned to Lord Jest. Tentatively, someone clapped. Then someone else. Soon, the tent was filled with applause.

"Thank you, thank you," Claude said shakily.

"They're not clapping for *you*," Lord Jest honked. He lifted his trunk proudly in the air. "They're clapping for me!"

A bead of sweat dripped its way down Claude's brow as he tried unsuccessfully to close his torn vest. "That, uh, amazing rescue was brought to you by our very own circus

elephant, Lord Jest!" he announced. He laughed nervously, tugging at his vest again. "Sorry if we got your heart racing a little there! But all's well that ends well, right? Especially at the circus! Now if you can all proceed to the exit in a calm and orderly fashion. And thanks again for coming to the Most Magnificent Traveling Circus, the show that, uh . . . keeps you on your toes!"

Claude kept a smile plastered on his face until the last of the guests had left. But as soon as the tent was empty, he marched backstage, his face contorting with fury. In the chaos of the fire, most of the employees had sprinted out of the tent, leaving only Lloyd, Loyd, and Susan waiting with the animals. The Nillings had been the first to leave, shouting wildly in their language as they pushed in front of each other to get to the exit. Susan had almost followed them, but then she'd looked back at the animals, shaking as they cowered away from the flames, and she found she just couldn't leave. "Lloyds! Susan! Bring the animals backstage," Claude barked. "NOW!"

Smalls felt a chain wrap around his neck. With a yank, Loyd jerked Smalls backstage. "YOU!" Claude burst out when he saw him. He spit a fingernail out at Smalls. "What happened out there, you worthless bear?" He lifted his foot, giving Smalls a swift kick to the stomach.

Smalls winced. "It wasn't my fault," he tried to tell Claude. "The whole fire stick went up in flames—"

Claude cut him off with another kick to the stomach. "Don't you growl at me, you WORTHLESS BEAR!"

"Stop it!" Tilda exploded. Smalls looked over at her in

193

surprise. She was trembling a little, but there was a fierce expression on her face as she glared up at Claude. "You . . . you big bully!"

"Quit that yapping!" Claude ordered. He kicked Tilda too, sending her skidding across the floor. Then for good measure, he kicked Wombat, who collided into Tilda. "No more squeaks or grunts or growls or"—his eyes landed on Rigby—"barks!"

Ducking out of his chain, Rigby ran over to Susan and leapt frantically into her arms. His legs splayed out on either side of her and with a yelp, he buried his head in her shoulder.

"Shhh," Susan whispered, staggering backward under his weight. "It's okay, Rigby." Shivering, Rigby peeked up at her through a mop of fur. His dark eyes were wide and round, and it struck Susan suddenly how young he seemed, not much older than a puppy. "I've got you," she told him. She tightened her grip on his back and slowly she felt his shivers start to subside.

Meanwhile, Claude was stomping angrily through the tent, kicking at anything—or anyone—that got in his way. "You vile, worthless animals," he seethed. "You've ruined everything! How am I ever going to sell the circus now? Ames sprinted out of here like the place was on fire. Oh, wait—because it WAS!" He shouted the last word, pounding on Lloyd's shoulder with his fist. "The whole finale was a . . . a . . ."

"Calamity?" Wombat offered as he pulled himself off Tilda.

"Disaster!" Claude finished.

Claude kept yelling, but Susan had stopped listening. What did Claude mean by *sell the circus*? She lifted one of her hands off Rigby's back. There was a clot of blood dried on it from where another blister had popped during her performance tonight. Did Claude really want to sell the circus? Hope lifted inside her like a balloon. Would that mean she could go home?

"Bertie!" Claude yelled, making Susan jump. He spun around, scanning the tent. "Boy!" he tried again. "Bring me Wilson!" But no one stirred in the tent.

Stay away, Bertie, Susan begged silently. The last thing Claude needed right now was that stick.

"BERTIE!" Claude tried once more. "BRING ME WILSON!" But still no small boy appeared backstage.

"Fine. Who needs him?" Claude gnawed on a fingernail, spitting it angrily at Juliet. She flinched as it landed on her muzzle, sliding off her nose. "Lloyd, Loyd, lock the animals back up in their cages," Claude continued. "No dinner for any of them tonight. Or," he added cruelly, "any meals tomorrow. These animals better get used to being hungry."

Lord Jest's trunk snapped up. "How 'bout the elephant, Boss?" He walked over to Claude, looking down at him pleadingly. "I saved the day for ya! I want my real dinner."

"Stop that awful honking, elephant. It's hurting my ears." Lifting his foot, Claude gave Lord Jest a hard kick. His shoe collided with an old wound on his trunk, and Lord Jest cried out as it split open again.

"But I saved the day," he said weakly. "I'm supposed to be the hero."

"I said NO HONKING!" Claude gave Lord Jest another kick, right in his open cut.

As blood trickled down Lord Jest's trunk, he ducked his head, whimpering softly.

"Worthless animals," Claude muttered. "All of them." Then he turned on his heels and stormed out of the tent.

Chapter Thirty-two

A Covert Op

Bertie stood inside a fold of the tent's curtain, Lord Jest's whimper ringing in his ears. His knuckles were white from clutching Wilson so tightly, and inside him, an argument was raging.

You have to do something, his heart was telling him.

You can't do something, his brain fought back. *It's not safe!*

But the animals need me, his heart replied.

And you need your limbs, his brain argued. *If Claude catches you . . .*

A succession of images flashed through Bertie's head. May's inflamed wound. Lord Jest's injured trunk. His own legs, wobbling uselessly after days in that cabinet.

He peeked out through the curtain. Claude was gone, and Lloyd and Loyd were dragging the animals out of the tent. Bertie flinched as he caught sight of the blood dripping down Lord Jest's trunk. Behind him, Smalls let out a strangled cough as Loyd tightened the chain around his neck, and Tilda shrieked as Lloyd lifted her into the air by a paw. Bertie squeezed Wilson even tighter, the cool metal of the stick cutting into his skin. It didn't matter what happened to him. He had to do something.

In the back of the tent, Loyd grabbed Rigby out of Susan's arms. "Get out of here, squirt," he said, giving Susan a shove. "The animals are my job." Susan kept her eyes on Rigby as she headed reluctantly toward the exit. But as she passed by the fold in the curtain, she caught sight of two bright blue eyes peeking out. She stopped short, staring at Bertie. He held a finger to his lips, signaling for her to be quiet.

"Is there a problem, squirt?" one of the Lloyds asked sharply.

"No," Susan said quickly. She hurried on to the exit, but when the Lloyds weren't watching, she glanced over her shoulder at Bertie.

Kitchen, he mouthed. Claude used to keep the kitchen caravan locked up tight, but during a storm last month, the lock had broken—and he had yet to replace it. *Meet you there,* he added. Susan gave him a tiny nod before slipping out of the tent.

Bertie waited until the Lloyds had led all the animals out

of the tent before emerging from his hiding spot. Taking Wilson with him, he dashed outside. He didn't break until he'd reached the kitchen caravan. But in front of the door, he paused, his stubborn brain flaring up once again.

If Claude finds you . . . it began.

Bertie didn't give it time to finish. He flung open the door, stepping inside. Susan was waiting with her back pressed up against the wall. "I've never been part of a covert op before," she said with a grin. "What are we doing here?"

"Food," Bertie declared. "We need food for the animals. And something to clean out Lord Jest's wound. And," he added, eying a streak of dried blood on Susan's palm. "Yours."

Susan went over to the sink, running soapy water over her palm. "Better," she said. "I keep thinking I'll work up the courage to ask Claude for ointment, but not today." She shook her head. "Did you hear him in there, Bertie? He was . . . out of control."

Bertie crouched down, rummaging through the cabinets. They were smaller than the ones in the supply caravan, and he tried not to think of what it would be like to be locked in one.

Susan began soaping up a washcloth for Lord Jest. "And he said something about selling the circus!" she said.

Bertie nodded. "I heard." A scene played out in his head suddenly: Claude leaving the circus and forcing Bertie to come with him, somewhere with no Susan and no Smalls, only Claude, morning, noon, and night. "You don't really think he would do that, do you?"

Susan draped the soapy washcloth over her shoulder. "I don't know why he would." She walked along the length of the train, looking thoughtful. "Didn't your grandfather start this circus? *His* father?"

"He did, but it's been Claude's for almost ten years now. And I think he's hated it for just as long." In the back of one of the cabinets, Bertie's hand closed around a jar. He pulled it out. It was a jar of peanut butter, still half full. Claude fed the animals peanut butter when he thought they'd performed exceedingly well—which was rarely. This jar had lasted a year already and would probably last another if Claude had anything to do with it.

Which he won't, Bertie decided. Behind the peanut butter was a sack of carrots—old, but not so old they'd grown mold yet. "Perfect," he said triumphantly. "I've got the food."

"And I've got the washcloth." Susan paced distractedly to the other side of the caravan. "Don't you think it's strange that Claude would bring in all these new animals if he's trying to sell the circus? It's almost as if he brought them in to *help* sell the circus." She walked faster, pacing back and forth. "What if he did? Maybe—"

Before she could finish that thought, her foot smashed into a loose floorboard. "Ow!" She grabbed her foot in her hand, hopping up and down. "Ow, ow, ow!"

As Bertie ran over to help her, something on the ground caught his eye. The floorboard. She'd dislodged it with her foot. It was now sticking up in the air, revealing a fabric-lined compartment hidden underneath. "Susan, look." Kneeling on the ground, he pulled the floorboard up the rest of the way.

Susan crouched down next to him, forgetting all about her foot. "A hiding spot," she said excitedly, leaning in. Nestled inside the compartment was what looked to be a jewelry box. It was made of dark mahogany wood and had a checkered pattern inlaid across the top. Susan reached down, running her finger along the top of it. She knew that box.

Her dad had made it for her mom years ago. He'd carved her name across the front: PAULA, in sweeping, curling letters. Her mom had stored spoons in it, keeping it on a ledge in the kitchen. But not long before Susan had been sent off to work at the circus, her mom had given it to her as a gift. She'd even had Susan's dad add her name to the other side: SUSAN, in the same sweeping, curling letters. "For you, no

spoons," she'd told Susan. "One day you will have jewelry to put in this box."

Like almost everything else, Susan had been forced to leave it when she joined the circus. With shaky hands, she pulled out the box. Right away she saw it: the letters of her name, curling across the side.

"It's yours?" Bertie asked softly.

"It was," she said. "Once." She tried to open the top, but it was locked. There was a hole for a key in the front, and she vaguely remembered the skeleton key that went to it, long and bronze, with a handle that looped and curved. She gave the box a shake, and something jostled lightly inside. It wasn't empty.

"Why would he hide it from me?" she murmured. "And why would he lock it?" She stood up abruptly, hugging the box to her chest. She had to get it open. She had to find out what was inside.

"Claude keeps all his keys on a chain next to his bed," Bertie said.

Susan looked over at him in surprise. He was smiling at her, a mischievous look in his eyes. Gently, he removed the washcloth from her shoulder. "Go," he said, nodding toward the door.

Susan hugged the box even tighter. "You'll be okay?"

"Food and washcloth," Bertie said, holding them out to show her. "I've got it covered."

She nodded. "Thank you," she said softly. Then, with the box pressed against her, she jumped down from the caravan.

Behind her, Bertie closed up all the cabinets, making sure everything was exactly how he'd found it. He was just finishing up when something in the corner of the caravan caught his eye. Another floorboard, warped from years of wear, was poking up at the corner the slightest bit.

Suddenly, he had an idea. Hurrying over to the floorboard, he crouched down on the ground and began yanking at it with all his might. After a few seconds, the floorboard came loose with a loud creak. Bertie broke into a smile as he lifted it up. Underneath was a hole just large enough to conceal a long metal stick.

Picking up Wilson, Bertie shoved the stick into the compartment under the floor. Then he carefully fastened the floorboard over it again, giving it a good stomp to make sure it was tightly in place. *"Ha,"* he said, smiling widely. "Let Claude find you there."

Chapter Thirty-three
Buck Is at Your Service

Back in their cages, the animals were hungry, and they were grumpy.

"I'm too hungry to sleep," Rigby groaned.

"I'm too hungry to clean," Tilda sighed.

"I'm too hungry to *think*," Wombat chimed in.

"Stop your whining already!" Lord Jest snapped. "You're not the ones who spent all your time planning a sabotage, just to—" Suddenly he stopped short. "Never mind," he said quickly. But it was too late.

"Sabotage?" Smalls asked slowly. It was a Wombat kind of word, a word that made you stop and think.

In her cage, Juliet leapt to her feet. *"Sabotage?"* she repeated.

"My fire sticks," Smalls said as it dawned on him. "You did something to my fire sticks to make them burst into flames!"

Lord Jest shrugged his trunk. "It might be possible your fire sticks found their way into the vat of oil at the concession stand," he admitted, unable to keep a note of pride from creeping into his voice.

"My tightrope." Wombat's ears shot straight up. "You used oil to grease it, didn't you? I knew I wasn't to blame for my faux pas!"

"And you put mud in my top hat," Tilda wailed. She looked miserably down at her soiled fur. "I'm going to have to go through my sixteen-step grooming process at least sixteen *times* to get this out!"

"The hole in my beach ball," Rigby chimed in, sounding bewildered. "That was from *you*?"

Lord Jest twirled his trunk. "So what if it was?"

"Hey, the hole in the ball was my idea," Buck protested.

"You were part of this, Buck?" Juliet slapped her tail angrily against the bars of her cage. "Why would you do that?"

"They were getting too good, Juliet," Buck said. "You saw the bear. He was doing the hardest trick in the circus, and he was *nailing* it."

"We were trying to get more food for the Lifers," Lord Jest declared.

"And instead you got us all starved," Hamlet replied.

"At least we *tried* something," Buck argued. "Though

for the record, pretty puff," he told Tilda, "I was all for putting a little oil in your hat instead. I said, why mess up that pretty fur when we can just make her slip and fall? But if you need any help cleaning, Buck is at your service."

Wombat rushed to the front of his cage. "You will be nothing of the sort," he declared angrily. "If Tilda needs any services, I, Fred, her *boyfriend*, will provide them! Can you comprehend that, Buck?" He paused, glaring at the zebra. "What kind of name is Buck, anyway?" he went on. "It's better suited for a chipmunk than a zebra! I don't see any buckteeth on you, *BUCK*!"

"That's enough, Wombat." Tilda's voice was the sharpest Smalls had ever heard it. "I think you're overreacting!"

"Overreacting?" Wombat huffed. "I apologize if I don't like that *chipmunk* offering you his services!" He flopped down on his stomach, sulking.

Across the way, Juliet shook her head. "I just can't believe you did this, Buck," she said. "It doesn't matter who they are. It's beneath you."

"Don't tell me you're starting to *care* about them, Jul," Buck groaned.

"Of course not," Juliet said sharply.

"Ya know what I say," Lord Jest offered. "Caring only gets ya in trouble."

As the Lifers argued on one side of the caravan and Tilda and Wombat argued on the other side, Smalls rested his head against the wall of his cage. He knew he should be mad at Lord Jest—furious, even—but suddenly he just felt sad for him. To go through your whole life refusing to care for anyone. . . . It made Smalls feel hollow, like his insides had been scooped out and scraped clean.

"Rigby?" he called out.

"Yeah, Smalls?" Rigby called back.

"Just making sure you're still there."

Rigby laughed. Smalls could just make out the faint sound of his tail swishing against the floor of his cage. "Where else would I be?"

Smalls closed his eyes, comforted by that. *At least*, he thought, *we're all in this together*.

Chapter Thirty-four

Better Than Fuchsia Ice Cream

"I want the circus tent to be so sparkling clean, I can see my reflection in the floor."

At the sound of Claude's voice, Bertie dove into the shadows behind the animals' caravan. Fear cut through him as he looked down at the stolen food in his hands.

"I want every nook and cranny polished," Claude went on. Bertie heard three sets of footsteps coming closer. He pressed up against the caravan, trying to sink into the shadows. "I want every last speck of ash gone. I want every hole glued up. I want every burn painted over. Understood, boys?"

"Absolutely!" one of the Lloyds said.

"Definitely!" the other Lloyd added.

"And I want it done by practice time tomorrow," Claude continued.

"Practice?" one of the Lloyds spit out at the same as his brother cried, *"Tomorrow?"*

"Is there a problem with that?" Claude asked coolly. He was close enough now that Bertie could smell him: that sharp, sour Claude essence, like cheese gone bad, barely masked by his perfumed soap and the traces of cocoa that always clung to his breath. "Because I can find a new pair of twins if you prefer . . ."

"No, Boss," one of the Lloyds said faintly.

"We'll take care of it, Boss," the other Lloyd added.

"Good. Now go. There are only twelve hours until practice. And," Claude muttered under his breath, "I am in dire need of my cocoa nightcap."

Bertie waited until their footsteps faded into the distance before creeping out from behind the caravan. With Claude, Lloyd, and Loyd gone, the grounds were eerily quiet. *I did it,* he thought as he slipped into the animals' caravan. Claude had been there, so close he could smell him, and Bertie hadn't been found. It made him feel like he could do anything.

As Bertie clicked the door shut behind him, the caravan came alive with activity. The animals all rushed to the fronts of their cages. "That PB has my name on it," Lord Jest said. He stuck his trunk through the bars of his cage, trying to pluck the jar out of Bertie's hands.

"Whoa." Bertie laughed. "Don't worry, Lord Jest. You'll get plenty." He waved the sack of carrots through the air, watching as all eight animals followed it with their eyes. "You all will."

Smalls's stomach growled loudly at the sight of the food. He'd eaten peanut butter once before. It was as sticky as honey but thicker, the kind of food that filled in your holes and stuck to your ribs. Bertie moved quickly through the caravan, dispensing peanut butter–dipped carrots to each of the animals.

"I've never tasted anything quite as delicious in my life," Wombat declared, all traces of sulking gone from his voice.

"It tastes even better than fuchsia-colored strawberry ice cream," Rigby agreed—but the peanut butter stuck to his tongue, making it sound more like "itjaskievnbrrrthafusiiicrm."

"Just be careful not to get it on your paws, boys," Tilda lectured. "Peanut butter is impossible to clean out of your fur."

Bertie stopped at Smalls's cage last. "I saw the finale," he said quietly as he slipped a carrot into Smalls's cage, slathered top to bottom in peanut butter. Smalls gobbled it down in one bite. It stuck right to his ribs, like he knew it would, but it did little to fill the holes inside him. He wished he could explain to Bertie what happened, tell him that awful word: *sabotage*. But he couldn't.

"I'm sorry," Bertie said, feeding Smalls another carrot. "Something was wrong with that fire stick." He shook his head. "I should have checked them beforehand."

"*I'm* sorry," Smalls argued. "I should have known Lord Jest would try something like that. I should have been ready somehow."

"But we've got another show tomorrow night," Bertie went on, scratching Smalls under his chin. "We'll show them what you can do then, right, Smalls?"

"Wah, wah, wah," Lord Jest interrupted. "You two sound like a buncha crybabies. Stop gabbing already! There's an elephant over here who's dying for more peanut butter."

"I think Lord Jest is still hungry," Bertie said with a laugh. "That or he's got something up his trunk."

"He's got something up his trunk all right," Smalls said, glaring at Lord Jest. But as Bertie fed him another peanut butter–dipped carrot, Smalls started to feel better. *Tomorrow*, he thought. It was a word with depth and layers, a word that could be peeled away, strip by strip, until you got to the nugget of possibility at the center. Tomorrow he had another chance.

"All right, Lord Jest, I'm coming," Bertie said playfully. "I know you've got a big stomach to fill."

"You betcha I do," Lord Jest said, smacking his trunk in anticipation.

Bertie sat down in front of Lord Jest's cage, feeding him several more peanut butter–dipped carrots. When the carrots finally ran out, he pulled the soapy washcloth out of his pocket. "Let's clean out that wound, okay?" he said. "We don't want a repeat of what happened to May."

An image of May flashed through his mind; he imagined her looking plump and healthy, hooting loudly as she swung from one banana tree to another. "Unless we could find a sanctuary for you too," he said softly. He reached into Lord Jest's cage, cradling his trunk in his arms. "This is going to make it better," he promised. Gently, he began cleaning Lord Jest's wound with the washcloth. Lord Jest whimpered, trying to pull his trunk away, but Bertie held on tight.

"I know," he said soothingly. "But it has to be done." He kept talking as he cleaned out the wound, his tone soft and reassuring. Slowly, Lord Jest's whimpers faded, and his trunk relaxed in Bertie's arms.

Smalls furrowed his brow as he watched Lord Jest. Leaning against the bars of his cage, his trunk hanging loose in Bertie's arms, Lord Jest looked almost *calm*. As the elephant murmured, "That feels better," and looked down at Bertie,

Smalls could swear he saw something soften in his eyes. But then he looked back up, straight at Smalls. "Whatcha staring at?" he snarled. And just like that, his eyes were cold and hard again.

"Nothing," Smalls said. "Nothing at all."

Chapter Thirty-five

A Bronze Key

Susan was standing outside Claude's caravan, clutching the wooden box in her hands. Just a minute ago, Claude had stormed inside, mixed himself a jug of hot cocoa, and then stormed back out, muttering something under his breath. The coast was clear now. All she had to do was get inside and find the key before Claude returned. Easy. Simple. She just wished her pulse would quit racing.

She glanced over her shoulder one more time. But she saw nothing but darkness, stretching on to the horizon. *It's now or never*, she thought. She sprinted to the door. The handle was cool and slippery in her grip. She closed her eyes as she flung the door open, as if somehow that could make her invisible. Two steps and she was inside, pulling the door shut behind her.

It took a second for her pulse to slow. Her palms had

gotten all sweaty in the dash, so she wiped them on her skirt, wincing a little as the fabric rubbed at a raw blister. But as she looked around, she forgot about the pain. "Wow," she murmured. She'd never been inside Claude's caravan before, and she couldn't help but gape a little.

Everything in Claude's caravan must have been beautiful once: the velvet sofa, the lion-clawed table, the long counter lined with jugs and urns and tins. But it was all old and worn now, the sofa torn, the table stained, the tins dented. It made her think of a sand castle after it had been washed over by the ocean: a shadow of its former self. But still, it was *big*. She thought of the tiny cubby she slept in, barely large enough to fit her straw sack of a bed.

"I should start sleeping on this couch," she muttered as she pushed her way through a crystal beaded curtain to get to the bedroom. On the right side of Claude's bedroom was his closet. Twice the size of her cubby, it was lined with outfits in every shade of the rainbow, with a whole section just for shades of gold. Along the back wall, lined up meticulously, were Claude's top hats. There were all kinds: short, tall, satin, velvet, with beaded and feathered and sequined brims. *A hat for every outfit,* Susan had heard Claude brag once.

On the other side of the room was Claude's bed—which

was about ten times the size of hers. His pajamas hung off the bottom, a black velvet set with circus images embroidered in gold: tents and trapezes and tightropes galore. Next to the bed was a small wooden nightstand, littered with earplugs and an old sleeping mask and an empty jug of cocoa.

Hanging off the chipped porcelain knob of the nightstand, Susan found what she looking for: a chain, crowded with keys. She reached for it excitedly, flipping quickly through the keys. They were jumbled together and unmarked, making it impossible to tell which went to what. But at the very bottom, beneath a clump of small silver keys, she spotted it. A bronze skeleton key, with a handle that curved and looped. "Bingo," she whispered, sliding the key off the chain.

She was just turning to leave when something sticking out of the nightstand's drawer caught her eye. It was the edge of a piece of paper. *Something to paint on*, Susan thought eagerly. She glanced over her shoulder. The caravan was still, no Claude in sight. Holding her breath, she slowly opened the drawer. But it wasn't a sheet of paper she found inside. It was a stack of old-fashioned photos. Susan's heart pounded as she picked them up. They were all of the same little boy. She paused on an image of the boy with a stern-looking older man. *Claude with his father,* someone

had written on the back. Susan gasped. The little boy in the photos was Claude.

The very last photo in the stack was worn thinner than the rest, as if it had been handled many times. In it, young Claude has his arm slung around a baby elephant. On the back was another note. Susan's eyes widened as she read it. She *had* to show this to Bertie! Folding the photo in half, she quickly tucked it into the waistband of her skirt. Then, shoving the rest of the photos back into the drawer, she hurried out of the caravan, locked box and key in hand.

Chapter Thirty-six

The Most Miserable Traveling Circus

Claude paced back and forth through the empty kitchen caravan. "You should never stop searching for the next big thing, son," he mimicked. "Magnificent can always become more magnificent!" Claude shook his fist at the ceiling. "Well, Father, I took your advice! And look what happened. Magnificent can also become miserable!"

Reaching into the very back of the tallest cupboard in the kitchen, Claude pulled out a half-eaten chocolate bar. With a sigh, he slid to the ground, stretching his long legs out in front of him. "The Most Miserable Traveling Circus," he mumbled, stuffing a chunk of chocolate into his mouth. "And it's all the fault of those Misfits," he continued, sending several chocolate bits tumbling to the ground. "Ames Howard will never buy the circus now!"

Standing back up, he pounded his fist angrily against

the counter. As he did, a single cabinet door creaked open. Claude furrowed his brow. Swallowing down the rest of his chocolate bar, he stalked over to the cabinet and peered inside. It was empty.

"The peanut butter," Claude said slowly. "And the carrots." He leaned in closer, squinting. Along the edge of the cabinet was a line of dust. And imprinted in that dust was a single fingerprint. He stood back up, stroking his beard. "Interesting," he said.

Meanwhile, on the other side of the circus grounds, Bertie kneeled behind the Big Top, digging a hole in the dusty ground. He'd decided it was the best way to cover up the evidence of his crime: a jar that had once held peanut butter and a sack that had once held carrots. Feeding the animals had left him feeling good, giddy, and he dug quickly, burning off the energy stirring inside him. He couldn't stop thinking about how the animals had all leapt to the front of their cages when he'd shown up with the peanut butter. The way they'd looked at him as they'd gobbled it down . . . it was almost as if he was some kind of hero.

"Bear Boy," he said. "The Peanut Butter Bandit." He smiled to himself. It had a nice ring to it.

He was almost finished with the hole when suddenly he heard it: heavy, clomping footsteps, the kind of footsteps that were made by shiny, hard-soled shoes. Bertie froze. Claude.

"There you are, boy," Claude said, stalking up behind him. "I've been looking for you everywhere."

"Hello, Uncle," Bertie said without turning around. Thinking fast, he shoved the empty food containers into the hole he'd dug, then whirled around, dropping down on top of it cross-legged. "Just taking in the view," he said casually. "It's a beautiful night, don't you think?" He glanced up at the sky, where not a single star was shining through a thick haze of fog. "I just, uh, love fog," he added quickly.

Claude narrowed his eyes suspiciously. "Any particular reason you chose this patch of dirt to sit on?"

Bertie racked his brain. "It's, uh, very soft," he said. He patted the ground next to him. "Really, you should give it a try."

Claude made a sour face. "Dignified men don't sit on the *ground*." He circled Bertie, stroking his beard. "You know, it's peculiar, boy. I was in the kitchen caravan a few minutes ago when I noticed a jar of peanut butter and a sack of carrots missing. You wouldn't know anything about that." He stopped suddenly in front of Bertie, staring down at him. "Would you?"

"I wouldn't," Bertie said quickly, averting his eyes.

"Are you sure?" Claude grabbed Bertie's chin, jerking

his head up until Bertie had no choice but to look directly at him.

"I'm sure," Bertie croaked, attempting a weak smile.

"Of course you wouldn't," Claude said, shoving Bertie's chin away. "I don't know what I was thinking. You're not brave enough to do something like that." He laughed loudly. "I should thank my lucky stars that you're a weak little boy. Now get to your room! Little boys shouldn't be wandering around at night. Especially not ones who have to get up three hours early tomorrow to scrub the Big Top with a toothbrush."

"What?" Bertie burst out.

"That's what happens," Claude told him, "when your bear chooses to freeze up during the most IMPORTANT SHOW OF MY LIFE!" Claude coughed, taking a second to compose himself. "You can also count on skipping breakfast tomorrow. As well as lunch. And while we're at it, dinner." He smiled lightly as he turned to leave. "I'll have to starve the other workers as well," he muttered to himself. "Until somebody finally admits they stole that food."

"No!" The word shot right out of Bertie. It felt exactly like he'd always thought it would—like a bullet, aimed right at Claude. But different too. Freeing. What had he been so afraid of all these years? "No!" he said again, loving the way it slid off his tongue. "No, no, no!"

Slowly, Claude turned around again. "What did you say to me, boy?"

"I said *no*," Bertie repeated. "You will not starve the other workers." He took a deep breath, standing up to reveal the hollow jar and empty sack beneath him. "Because I'm the one who stole the food." He looked right into Claude's eyes. "The animals deserved to eat."

Claude blinked several times as he stared back at him. "You," he said slowly. "You . . . ungrateful, vile, WASTE OF A LITTLE BOY!" He chewed furiously on a fingernail, spitting it out at Bertie. It landed on Bertie's hand, and he quickly slipped it into his pocket to add to his jar.

"For years, I've fed you," Claude went on. "For years, I've clothed you. For years, I've housed you. And this is how you repay me. By stealing from me! You are worthless," Claude said. "WORTHLESS! And now you will have to work twice as hard to pay me back for this theft."

Bertie looked down at his torn shirt and his dirty suspenders. He thought about the dry, hard oats he ate every meal and the straw-filled burlap sack he called a bed and the tiny storage closet he was forced to sleep in. "No," he said suddenly. "I won't." The words spiraled around him like a tornado, sweeping him up in their power.

"*No?*" Claude sputtered.

"No," Bertie repeated. "Because I'm leaving." He stood up taller. "I'm going to find my mom. I don't care if she's sick. I don't care if she's lost her mind! I'll take care of her. I'm not a little boy anymore!"

"Your mom?" Claude burst out laughing.

"Yes," Bertie said defiantly. "My mom. My *real* family."

Claude shook his head. "You'll do no such thing, boy." He moved closer to Bertie, until Bertie could smell the cocoa on his breath. "Because your mom is dead."

Bertie took a step back. He felt like he'd been kicked in the stomach by Lord Jest, like he'd had the breath stomped right out of him. "What?" he whispered.

"Your mom is dead," Claude repeated matter-of-factly. "She has been for years."

"B-but my money . . ." Bertie stammered. "You've been putting it away so I can visit her!"

Claude chewed another fingernail, spitting it out at Bertie. This time, Bertie let it tumble to the ground. "That's the beauty of it. I haven't. All along you've been working for me for free, and you were too worthless to realize it."

Bertie couldn't breathe. The world was upside down and inside out and he couldn't tell anymore if he was standing or falling. "No," he said again. "No!"

Claude smiled thinly. "Yes," he said. "Yes."

Chapter Thirty-seven

A New Purse for Chrysanthemum

"I'm feeling goooood," Buck said, scuffing a hoof against the floor of his cage. "A full stomach from something other than slop! I haven't felt this good in ages. I bet I'm looking pretty good too, aren't I, my little nuzzle bunny?" He puckered his lips at Tilda, revealing his very pink gums.

Tilda, who was on her fifth round of her sixteen-step grooming process, looked up with a grimace.

"Too bad we can't share a cage," Buck continued. "Then you could show me just *how* good I look." He made a kissing noise, then pretended to blow it over to Tilda. "Mwah mwah mwah, my beautiful butterball."

"What do you think you're doing?" Wombat exploded. He glared furiously at Buck. "She's *my* girlfriend! What don't you understand about that?" He raised his voice until it boomed through the caravan, rattling the cages. "MINE!"

"Stop it, Wombat!" Tilda's shout took every animal in the caravan by surprise. All heads turned in her direction. "Both of you stop it RIGHT NOW!"

"*Tilda?*" Wombat gasped.

"*Bunny love?*" Buck gasped.

Tilda fluffed out her freshly cleaned fur. "Yes," she said. "It's me, and I want both of you to listen and listen closely. My name is Tilda. Not 'sweet thing,' not 'honey bunny,' not 'butterball—'"

"You tell him, Tilda!" Wombat interrupted.

"Silence!" Tilda bellowed. "*I* am talking now."

"Fine," Wombat muttered, sulking to the back of his cage.

"As I was *saying*," Tilda went on. "I am Tilda, not 'nuzzle bunny,' not 'bunny buns,' and not 'girlfriend.' *Tilda*. And I don't belong to anyone!"

Wombat's head snapped up. "Not even to me?" he asked softly.

"Not even you." Tilda lifted her fluffy white head in the air. "I am my own bunny. I speak for myself. And most importantly, I make my own decisions! And here is my decision." She cleared her throat. "Buck?" she said loudly.

"Yes?" Buck stuck his nose eagerly through the bars of his cage, giving his tail a seductive swish.

"Buck," Tilda continued bravely. "My heart belongs to someone else. His name is Wombat, even though he seems to think it's Fred, and he's the kindest, smartest, most wonderful animal I've ever known." In his cage, Wombat perked up. "You, on the other hand," Tilda continued, "are nothing more than a buffoon!"

"That's right!" Wombat burst out. "You tell him, Tilda! He's nothing but a big, tall, striped *buffoon!*"

"Enough, Wombat," Tilda said angrily. "You know I love you, but you've been acting pretty buffoonish yourself lately. Now let me finish!"

Wombat snapped his mouth shut, looking shaken.

"A buffoon?" Buck asked indignantly. "Look at my stripes, sweet thi—ahem, *Tilda*." He ruffled his black and white mane. "I'm no buffoon. I'm a purebred zebra!"

"You are," Tilda agreed. "But you're also a buffoon. And I would never, ever, in a million, trillion years, even if we were the last two animals on earth, even *consider* dating you!"

On the other side of the grounds, while Tilda was busy yelling, Claude was busy grumbling. *"No,"* Claude muttered to himself as he stalked back to his caravan. "The boy actually said *no* to the great Claude Magnificence. And then he just ran off!" He paused to bite off one of his nails, spitting it onto the ground. "Of all the gall! I'm going to have to think long and hard about a punishment for this one . . ."

He began ticking off possibilities on his fingers. "There's the cabinet . . . no." He shook his head. "Not nearly severe enough. There's always sleeping with the animals . . . no, that worthless boy would probably *like* that."

"Excuse me?"

At the sound of a woman's voice, Claude fell abruptly silent. He turned around to find a pale-faced woman in an expensive-looking suit and a young girl in a poufy yellow dress walking toward him. The girl had wild brown curls and was swinging a small dollhouse between her hands. "Are you Mr. Claude Magnificence?" the woman asked.

Claude adjusted his gold top hat. "He is I," he said grandly.

"Oh, Mr. Magnificence, I'm so glad to meet you!" the woman gushed. "I'm Mrs. Toddle, and my daughter and I were at your, uh, very interesting show tonight."

Claude threw his shoulders back, making his torn vest pop open. "Very good," he said in his most formal voice.

"And you see," Mrs. Toddle continued, "my daughter seems to have formed an attachment to that dirty little rabbit that fell out of your top hat."

"She's an Angora rabbit," the girl informed her mother.

"Lauren Nicola showed me her picture in the paper the other day and she has the most beautiful white fur in the world, prettier than even my prettiest silk coat! When *he* isn't covering her in mud, that is." She shot Claude an accusatory look.

"I assure you, the mud was quite accidental," Claude said quickly. "I'm actually not sure how it got there in the first place . . ." He trailed off, looking puzzled.

"It doesn't matter," the girl cut in impatiently. She gave her dollhouse an angry shake. "I want her, Mother! I'm going to carry her everywhere with me instead of a purse. I will be the most fashionable girl in the world.

I will be more fashionable even than Lauren Nicola!" She paused to smooth down her yellow dress. "You *said* if I ate all my broccoli today, I could have whatever toy I wanted. And this," she went on, her voice rising shrilly, "is what I want!"

"Yes, yes, Chrysanthemum." Mrs. Toddle coughed nervously. "Just please don't shriek." She turned to Claude. "Tell me, Mr. Magnificence. How much for the rabbit?"

Claude stroked his beard as he stared at her. "You want to buy my rabbit?"

"That's right," Mrs. Toddle said. "I'll pay top dollar for her. My little girl only eats her vegetables if we give her a new toy every day. Usually she simply takes one from our store—we own Toddle's Toy Emporium, you see, I'm sure you've heard of it—but when she saw your rabbit tonight, she just had to have it. We were almost home when she made me turn the car around to come back here." She laughed, patting Chrysanthemum on the head. The girl quickly swatted her hand away. "Such a strong-willed girl, my Chrysanthemum is! So tell me, Mr. Magnificence. How much for the rabbit?"

"You'll pay top dollar, you say?" A greedy look crept onto Claude's face. He pulled a napkin and pen out of his pocket and scribbled down a number. "This is my price," he said, slipping the napkin to the Mrs. Toddle.

"That's very high," she gasped.

"She's a very valuable rabbit," Claude replied. "Purebred Antorka, just like your daughter said."

"Angora," the girl corrected rudely.

Claude waved a hand dismissively through the air. "Potato, patato. That's my price," he said. "Take it or leave it."

"We'll take it," Chrysanthemum proclaimed. She grabbed the napkin from her mom and tossed it onto the ground without even looking at it. "Won't we, Mother?" she added, her voice rising shrilly again.

"Yes," Mrs. Toddle said quickly. "Just please don't shriek, Chrysanthemum." She pulled a checkbook out of her purse and quickly wrote a check out to Claude. "We want the rabbit," she said, handing it to him.

Claude bounced excitedly on the toes of his shiny gold shoes as he looked down at the check. "Magnificent," he said. "I'll be right back. I must get the keys from my caravan. And," he added under his breath, "put this check where no one will find it." He took off at a sprint without looking back.

Inside his caravan, he opened his cocoa urn and slid the check inside. "You should be safe there, my sweet," he told the check lovingly. Placing the top back on the urn, he hurried through the crystal beaded curtain to his bedroom. He paused in front of his night table, eying his chain of keys, which hung a little crookedly from the knob. "Something looks different," he murmured. For a second, he just stood there, stroking his beard. Finally he shrugged. "Who cares? I'm rich!" He grabbed the chain off the nightstand. "Rich, rich, rich!"

The mother and daughter were in the middle of an argument about what vegetable Chrysanthemum would eat tomorrow when Claude reached them. Chrysanthemum had put down her dollhouse and was gesturing wildly as she told her mom that it didn't matter *what* toy she bought her, she was never, *ever* eating brussels sprouts.

"Good choice," Claude said magnanimously. "The brussels sprout is a very unfortunate vegetable." He clapped briskly. "Now, follow me to your new rabbit. I have plenty of other animals for sale too, if you're interested," he added as he led the Toddles to the animals' caravan.

"I only like Angora rabbits," Chrysanthemum sniffed. In her excitement, she forgot about her dollhouse, leaving it abandoned on the ground.

"Here we are!" Claude announced, flinging open the door to the caravan. He stomped over to Tilda's cage, where Tilda had, at that very moment, just finished yelling at Buck. He snatched her up, cringing as she let out an ear-piercing squeal. "Don't worry," he said, tossing Tilda to Chrysanthemum. "She's not usually this loud."

Chrysanthemum squeezed Tilda tightly in her arms. "You are going to be my very favorite toy," she announced. "I'm going to braid your hair and give you a million baths and bring you over to Lauren Nicola's house to show her that I'm the most fashionable girl in the world!"

"As I was saying, my other animals are for sale too," Claude said. He ran his hand temptingly down the row of cages. "For only double the price of the rabbit!"

Mrs. Toddle wrinkled her pale nose as she looked around the caravan. "No thank you," she said primly. "Come on, Chrysanthemum. Let's bring your new toy to the car. It smells like manure in here!"

Chrysanthemum squeezed Tilda tighter as she followed her mom outside. "And best of all," she went on, ignoring Tilda's strangled squeaks, "I'm going to tie a string around you and carry you around as my brand-new purse!"

Chapter Thirty-eight

Better Than Spoons
or Jewelry

Susan sat in her cubby, staring down at the box. On the other side of the caravan, she could hear the Nilling cousins jabbering away in their language as they tossed the occasional shoe at her curtain. But for once, she didn't care.

She gave the box another shake. It didn't clatter like spoons. It didn't jangle like jewelry. And it was much too light to be holding coins. What if it was nothing? Claude's receipts, maybe, or an extra reserve of cocoa powder? "Then it's nothing," she said out loud. "It's not a big deal." But her hand was shaking as she slid the key into the lock.

The box creaked a little as it opened. Inside were envelopes, dozens and dozens of them, jammed into every inch. Susan pulled one off the top. It was still sealed. *Susan Ward*, it said across the front. She pulled out another one, then another. They were all unopened, and they were all addressed to her.

She could barely breathe as she tore open one of the envelopes, yanking out a thin sheet of paper. *Dearest Susan,* she read. Her eyes jumped instantly to the signature at the bottom of the letter.

All our love,

Mom and Dad

Quickly, she opened up several more letters. The same signature stared back up at her each time. Susan felt like a horse was galloping across her chest. All those envelopes were letters. And they were all from her parents, for her. She rifled through the box, blowing out a breath as she checked the postmarked dates on the envelopes. Her parents had written her a letter almost every day she'd been at the circus. But why in the world would Claude keep them all, just to hide them from her? She shuddered at the thought of what he might be saving them for—some kind of awful bribe, most likely. But it didn't matter. Because she had them now, and she was never giving them back. Pulling her blanket around her shoulders, she began to read.

Dearest Susan,

It's been a month now, and we're starting to doubt that our letters are reaching you. We can only hope that they are and that, although you don't write back, one day you will show up on our doorstep, returned

*to us. You have to believe us that when we gave Mr.
Magnificence our permission for you to work at the
circus so we could pay off our debt, we knew nothing of
his plans to take the circus on the road. For as long as
we could remember, the Most Magnificent Circus had
been right down the road from us! If we had known,
oh, how quickly we would have rejected his offer! But
by the time we learned of his plans, the circus was gone,
and we were left with only a post office box to write to.
Every day we save a little more, and one day we hope
to have enough money to come find you and bring you
home. Until then, know you have—*

All our love,

Mom and Dad

Tears were brimming in Susan's eyes as she finished reading the letter. Blinking them away, she rummaged through the dates on the envelopes again. She found what she was looking for stuffed into the very back of the box: an envelope postmarked only days ago. Pulling it out, she eagerly tore it open.

Dearest Susan, she read.

*We believe we've made a new stride in finding you!
We've learned of one of the venues the Most Magnificent
Circus stops at each year, several hours north of us.*

*Soon we should have enough money saved up to travel
there. If we find you, we are not leaving without you—
we promise you that. We don't care if we have to give
up our farm or our home or anything else. We don't
want any of it if we can't have you. Until then, know
you have—*

All our love,
Mom and Dad

The letter slipped out of Susan's hands, fluttering to the ground. Her parents wanted her. They'd always wanted her. They *still* wanted her. She closed her eyes. Her whole body was trembling, but she'd never felt better. It was like for months she'd been in the dark, and suddenly the sun was shining again.

"They want me." It felt even better to say it out loud. Taking a deep breath, she pulled out another envelope. She'd stay up all night if she had to; she was going to read every last letter in that box.

Chapter Thirty-nine
A Buffoonish Wombat

"Buffoon?" Buck ruffled his mane. "I can't believe that itty-bitty bunny called me a buffoon! Who needs her anyway?" He kicked the wall with his hoof. "Not us! Right, *Fred*?"

Wombat stood motionless in his cage, staring blankly ahead of him. "She's gone," he whispered.

Smalls leaned against the wall that separated him from Wombat. "Are you all right, Wom—Fred?"

"Buffoonish," Wombat repeated. "She called me buffoonish. And my first thought was, '*Buck's* the buffoonish one, not me!'" He gasped. "I *have* been acting buffoonish!" He shook his head dismally. "Tilda was right. I was childish and cantankerous and worst of all, *jealous*. I was completely buffoonish! And now she's gone. And I can't even tell her I'm sorry." With a sad growl, he slumped down in his cage.

Smalls sat back on his haunches, rubbing at the yellow horseshoe on his chest. That terrible girl in yellow had called Tilda a toy, as if she was something to be played with, to be locked up in a trunk at the end of the day. An image of Tilda, locked at the bottom of a trunk, amidst cobwebs and dust bunnies, flashed through Smalls's mind. Until now, the one thing that had kept Smalls going was that they were all in this together, the four of them. But now, they didn't even have that. The idea of Tilda all alone tore at his heart.

"We have to find a way to get her back," he said.

"How?" Wombat asked miserably. "We're trapped."

Rigby swished his tail nervously across his cage. "We'd have to escape to do that," he said with a weak laugh.

Across the way, Buck stomped impatiently against the floor. "I've been talking to you over here, *Fred*. There are plenty more bunnies in the sea for us, right?"

Wombat looked up at Buck. "No," he said. "There aren't. At least not for me." He paused, his ears flicking forward. "And from now on, the name is Wombat," he decided. "Not Fred. If it's good enough for Tilda, it's good enough for me."

While Buck and Wombat were lamenting in their caravan, Tilda was being squeezed by Chrysanthemum in the backseat of a motorcar. "Squeak!" Chrysanthemum kept demanding, squeezing Tilda until she let out a strangled squeal. Chrysanthemum laughed in delight. "You're my new squeaky, high-fashion purse," she declared.

"First 'nuzzle bunny' and 'bunny buns' and now a *purse*?" Tilda burst out. "For your information, little girl, my name is Tilda!"

Chrysanthemum laughed at Tilda's squeaks, squeezing her even tighter. "Mother," she said. "I want to take my new purse to the store."

"*Now?*" Mrs. Toddle asked. She blinked her pale, watery eyes, stifling a yawn. "It's late, Chrysanthemum."

"I want to bring my purse to the store!" Chrysanthemum repeated, her voice rising shrilly. She shook her head, making her brown curls bounce up and down.

"Okay," Mrs. Toddle gave in. "We'll go to the store. Just please don't shriek."

Chrysanthemum smiled smugly to herself. "Works every time," she said under her breath.

A few minutes later, the motorcar turned down a long, narrow road. At the end of it, a building rose into the sky like a mountain. It was made of green brick and had a white lace trim and a white shingled roof that gave it the look of being snow-capped. A large sign became visible as the motorcar drew closer. TODDLE'S TOY EMPORIUM, it read.

Several unusual contraptions dotted the grassy area around the sign. There was a tall silver coil that sprinkled bits of candy into the air in random spurts. There was a boy built entirely of copper who was waving a rainbow of balloons in his copper hands. And nestled in a tall oak tree was a life-size version of the wooden dollhouse Chrysanthemum had left behind at the circus.

Chrysanthemum leaned back in her seat, a stray curl springing onto her forehead. "One day, Toddle's Toy Emporium will be all mine," she confided in Tilda. "I will be the first to own every toy that's ever invented." She looked out the window at the silver coil and the copper boy and the life-size dollhouse. "And I will be the only person in the world to own a Candy Springer and a Copper Boy and a Toddle's Original tree house. We'll see just how snooty Lauren Nicola is to me then!" She gave Tilda another tight squeeze, but this time, Tilda didn't feel it. Because curled up on Chrysanthemum's lap, the motorcar buzzing beneath her and Chrysanthemum's voice twisting above her, she'd fallen fast asleep.

Back in the caravan, the other animals had drifted off as well. "Tilda," Wombat kept murmuring in his sleep. Otherwise, the caravan was quiet, darkness washing over the cages like a lullaby. As everyone else slept on, Smalls sat back, absently touching the spot behind his ear where he used to keep his four-leaf clovers. He was just as tired as the others, but his mind refused to shut off. Something Rigby had said earlier had worked itself into the crevices of his brain, and no matter what Smalls did, he couldn't seem to get it out. "We'd have to escape to do that," Rigby had said.

It would be impossible, Smalls thought. *Or . . . would it?* Between Wombat's smarts and Rigby's imagination and his strength, why *couldn't* they do it? Excitement prickled at his paws. He turned in a circle, thinking hard. They'd have to find a time when they were out of their cages, of course. "When are we free?" he muttered to himself. "No cages or chains or Lloyds nearby . . ."

"Well, that's easy." Smalls jumped at the sound of Juliet's voice. He turned around to see her watching him curiously. "During the circus," she went on. "When we're out in the ring, performing for the audience. No cages or chains or Lloyds there."

Smalls snapped his head up. "Holy horseshoe," he murmured. She was right.

Juliet swished her tail thoughtfully, studying him. "Why were you asking about the cages anyway?"

"No reason," Smalls said, looking away. He had to admit that Juliet was starting to grow on him, but she was still a Lifer. "Just curious."

"Fine." Juliet shrugged. "Don't tell me." She lay down in her cage, trying to get comfortable. "It's not as if I care."

Chapter Forty
Worthless

That night, Bertie slept fitfully. He dreamed of a woman. Her back was to him, and he kept pleading for her to turn around. But every time she did, she would darken to ashes, scattering on the wind. By the time the light of dawn filtered through his tiny window and Claude flung his door open, Bertie felt like he'd barely slept a wink.

"Get out of bed, boy!" Claude ordered.

Bertie pulled his blanket tighter. "Why should I listen to you?" he mumbled into his pillow.

"I'll tell you why." Claude grabbed his arm, pulling him roughly out of bed. He crouched down until he was face-to-face with Bertie. "Because you're an orphan now, boy." The smell of hot cocoa poured off his breath. "You have no father. You have no mother. You have only me. Which means, like it or not, this is your home. And if you want to be fed, I suggest you get your skinny butt out to the Big Top and do your job."

He spit a fingernail in Bertie's face. "That bear you were supposed to train failed me yesterday! If he doesn't do better tonight, I've found a nice new home for you for the next few days. And believe me, it's going to make that cabinet in the supply caravan look like a mansion."

Bertie stared at him, not saying a word. *My mom is gone,* he thought. *Claude is all I have now.* Somewhere buried inside Bertie was a deep, deep sadness. But piled on top of it—heavier than bricks and steel and all the chains in the world—was anger. Anger so big and so black that it cast a shadow over everything.

Meanwhile, in the Big Top, Smalls was busy making lists.

Pros to Escaping

1. We could try to get Tilda back.

2. No more cages or rings or chains.

3. We'd never have to smell Claude's cocoa breath again.

Cons to Escaping

1. We could be caught.

2. We could be punished.

3. We'd have to leave Bertie.

Smalls sighed. Three versus three. He was getting nowhere.

As the door to the Big Top swung open, he looked over. In stalked Claude, with Bertie close at his heels. Bertie looked different, Smalls noticed. His muscles were tensed, and his eyes were distant, glazed, somewhere else altogether.

"Get to work, boy," Claude said, giving him a shove.

Bertie stumbled toward Smalls, his baseball cap slipping into his eyes. "We have to get this right today," he said sullenly. He pointed to Smalls's starting spot. "Start!" he ordered sharply.

Smalls cocked his head, confused. This boy looked like Bertie. He smelled like Bertie. But he was acting nothing like Bertie. Why wasn't he smiling? Or sneaking Smalls food? Or scratching him under the chin?

And then suddenly it hit Smalls. Bertie must be angry about his performance last night after all. Smalls's heart sank to his paws.

"Start!" Bertie ordered again. He pointed to Smalls's starting spot, and this time Smalls scrambled into his stance, anxious to please him. "We'll skip the hoop and just start with simple fire stick catching," Bertie said. "Since that's where things went so wrong yesterday." He tossed an unlit fire stick into the air. "One. Two. GO!" he commanded. But his voice was so curt that Smalls looked over at him in surprise—and completely missed the stick.

Bertie threw up his hands. "Come on, Smalls," he said, sounding exasperated. "That was an easy one!"

Smalls pawed the ground uneasily. He wished Bertie would just talk to him, tell him what was wrong. But Bertie wouldn't even look him in the eye.

The thing was, Bertie *couldn't* look Smalls in the eye. Because the anger inside him had grown so big that it was starting to swallow him whole. "Again," Bertie ordered, tossing another fire stick into the air. "One. Two. GO!"

This time, Smalls leapt forward, stretching out his tongue. But he was so desperate to please Bertie that he put too much force into it, and again he missed the stick completely.

Frustrated, Bertie gathered up the fire sticks. *This is my life,* he thought. He threw one of the sticks into the air. *This is all I have now.* He threw another one up. *I have no family.* He threw a third stick, then a fourth, not caring where they went. *I have no one. I am no one.* He threw a fifth stick without even looking. *I am worthless.* With all his might, he chucked the last stick into the air. "GO!" he yelled at Smalls.

Smalls leapt forward, trying to catch each of the six sticks as they spun wildly downward. But he had to move right as he moved left and forward as he moved back, and suddenly his feet were tangling and instead of catching, he was falling—all the way to the ground. The sticks smashed down around him, making *whack*ing noises as they hit the ground. The last one, the one Bertie had chucked upward so angrily, fell downward hardest, slicing through the air like a knife. But instead of hitting the ground near Smalls, instead of making the same *whack* as the other sticks, a gust of wind blew in from outside, pushing it toward Bertie. With a loud, angry *THWACK*, it slammed right into his head.

"Ow!" Bertie cried out. Pain shot through him, and again he thought those awful words. *I have no one. I am no one. I am worthless.*

The anger sucked him in, making him someone else entirely, someone hard and dark and wholly alone. When the words came out of his mouth, they belonged not to him, but to this darker, harder version. A person that was Bertie and wasn't Bertie, all at once. "YOU," he shouted at Smalls, "ARE. WORTHLESS!" Then he turned and he ran.

Chapter Forty-one

A Wooden Boy

Bertie didn't know where he was going. He just knew that he had to get away, and fast, somewhere where nothing could reach him, not even his feelings. *Susan's cave in the woods,* he thought suddenly—and that's where his legs steered him, pumping wildly as they kicked up dust in his wake.

His body moved automatically, as if that too didn't belong to him. He closed his eyes, letting his limbs take over. He was Invisible Boy, he told himself. He wasn't even there. No sooner had the thought crossed his mind than his foot collided with something hard. He lurched forward, waving his arms through the air to regain his balance. But it was too late. He landed on his stomach with his second *thwack* of the day. For several seconds, Bertie just lay there, his cheek pressing against the dusty ground.

In the distance, he could hear Claude yelling and Loyd—

or maybe it was Lloyd—saying, "Of course, Boss! You're right, Boss!" An image of Smalls flashed through Bertie's mind. The way he'd looked at him when he'd yelled . . . *No.* He blinked the image away.

With a groan, he pulled himself up—and found himself staring straight at a miniature house. It was carved of wood and meticulously painted, not a detail out of place. There were gray shingles on the roof, white shutters on the windows, and a sprinkling of painted daisies around the front stoop. For an instant, Bertie forgot about himself as he pulled it onto his lap.

Above the tiny wooden door was a latch. Carefully, Bertie tugged at it. The top half of the house lifted up, revealing a whole home underneath. He leaned in close, studying it. There was everything: a miniature bed and a miniature desk and a miniature stove and even miniature plates, set out on a miniature table. There was a whole miniature family sitting at the table too: a dad and a mom and three colorfully painted kids. Bertie scrunched up his forehead as he looked at one of the kids. It was a boy, with a smattering of freckles and a shock of red hair sticking out from underneath a tiny wooden baseball cap.

He picked the boy up, laying him out in his palm. Like everything else in the house, he was carved out of wood. He had arms and legs that moved forward and backward and a blue sweater and brown pants painted onto him. His face was painted on too, and every tiny detail—from the individual eyelashes to the dotting of freckles—was perfect. He had bright blue eyes, much like Bertie's own. And even though Bertie knew they were made out of paint, they were so lifelike that he almost expected them to blink up at him.

As Bertie stared at the wooden boy, something tugged at the corner of his mind. It was a memory, thin and translucent as a bubble. The boy reminded him of something from his past. But no matter how hard he fought for it, the memory stayed just out of his reach.

"Faster, you lazy wombat!" Claude's angry shout drifted over from the Big Top, shaking Bertie out of his thoughts. He put the wooden house on the ground and stood up abruptly. He was just about to drop the boy inside too when at the last minute, he slipped him into his pocket instead. Then, breaking back into a run, he let his legs carry him toward the woods.

Meanwhile, inside the Big Top, Smalls was speechless. Lloyd had taken over his training, and as Smalls leapt through the flaming hoop and caught fire stick after fire stick with his tongue, he thought only of Bertie and that word he'd called him. *Worthless.*

Maybe Bertie was right. Maybe he was worthless. He couldn't save the circus last night, after all. And he couldn't stop Tilda from being taken away. He looked over at Wombat, who was moping his way across the tightrope, and Rigby, who kept withdrawing into his fur whenever Loyd looked away. He'd always been the one who made sure his friends were happy, but now he was even failing at that.

A breeze blew into the Big Top, making Smalls turn around. Bertie had left the door to the tent hanging wide open, and outside, Smalls could see the barren, dusty ground extending in every direction. In the distance, a line of trees stretched across the horizon, and suddenly Smalls found himself imagining what it would be like to kick up his paws and run—away from the Big Top and away from the caravans and right into those woods. He shivered a little at the thought. He'd never really lived in the wild; none of them had. But as Lloyd took the fire sticks from him and shoved him toward the hoop, Smalls couldn't shake the idea.

Somewhere beyond those woods was Tilda. If he could save her, they'd all be together again; they'd all be happy. But it was as Rigby had said: the only way to do that was to escape. Smalls pawed nervously at the ground as he took his spot by the hoop.

He wasn't worthless. And he was going to prove it.

Chapter Forty-two

Brighter Than the North Star

"Escape?" Wombat said. "As in take flight? Bolt? Make a break for it?"

"Exactly," Smalls confirmed. Claude, Lloyd, and Loyd had left for a coffee break, and now he, Wombat, and Rigby were huddled together in the back of the ring, chains around their paws. "We're going to escape, and then we're going to find Tilda."

Wombat gave him a curious look. "Does this have something to do with Bertie calling you—?"

"Of course not!" Smalls cut him off. "It has to do with Tilda. And"—he shook a chained paw at him—"our freedom." It was a word he'd never thought much about before, but now it seemed to sparkle in his mind, brighter than the North Star. It blinded him from everything else, even—almost—Bertie.

"Escape," Wombat said again, nodding his snout. "If I

rescued Tilda, she'd be required to forgive me for my utmost buffoonish behavior." His voice grew softer. "And we'd be together again. Okay," he said. "I'm in. Let's escape."

"But what about Mumford?" Rigby asked. He spit out a strand of fur that had found its way into his mouth. "What if he finally finds the circus, and we're gone?"

Smalls steeled himself as he looked from Rigby to Wombat. This was it. He couldn't protect them any longer. They had to know. "Mumford knows exactly where we are," Smalls said. "He's known all along."

Wombat wrinkled up his snout. "What are you saying, Smalls?"

It all came out in a rush. "Mumford bet us in a card game against Claude. And then he lost us. He bet us away."

"Why would he do such an atrocious thing?" Wombat whispered.

Rigby ducked his eyes under his fur, letting out a soft whimper. "He's as bad as Claude."

"No." Smalls shook his head, thinking of the way Mumford had always been: how he'd brought Smalls home from an auction instead of chickens and how he'd used his train money to purchase Wombat and how he'd let Rigby's mom wander onto his farm to give birth to her litter. "I think he's just . . . human."

"Human is quite a confusing thing to be," Wombat said with a sigh.

An image of Bertie flashed through Smalls's mind—how distant his eyes had seemed when he'd yelled at him. "I think it is," he agreed.

Rigby shook his fur out of his eyes. "I'm glad I'm a Komondor dog," he decided. "Even if my fur is plain old white."

They were all quiet for a minute. Finally, it was Rigby who asked it. "So if we want to escape, the question is: how?"

Smalls sat back on his haunches. "I think I have an idea."

As Smalls, Wombat, and Rigby huddled closer, the Lifers lounged on the other side of the ring. "The humans should take coffee breaks every hour," Buck said, making himself comfortable.

"It's better than having to practice," Lord Jest agreed with a yawn.

"I think my new circus act is going to be napping," Hamlet chimed in. Letting out a contented sigh, he rested his head on his paws.

Ignoring the others, Juliet flicked her ears toward the back of the ring, where Smalls, Rigby, and Wombat were crouched together, whispering. "Something is going on," she murmured to herself. Pretending to sift around in the velvet floor with her nose, she inched closer to the Misfits. "Maybe someone dropped some food out here," she said loudly, but no one took any notice. She inched even closer.

"We'll have to do it during a show," Smalls was saying. "Out in the ring. That's the only time we're not in chains or a cage without the Lloyds or Claude right next to us."

"But how?" Rigby asked. "There will be hundreds of other hands there to catch us."

"A distraction," Wombat said thoughtfully. "We'll need an enormous distraction."

"Like a fire?" Smalls joked.

Wombat's head snapped up. "Like a fire," he repeated.

They all looked at each other. "No one would notice us running out if the tent was on fire again," Rigby said.

Juliet's yellow eyes widened. "You're planning to escape," she burst out. She'd inched even closer, and now she was standing only feet from the Misfits. "I *knew* you were up to something last night!" she told Smalls.

Smalls glanced nervously at the other Lifers, but they were all snoozing contentedly away. "Maybe we are," he said defensively. "What does it matter to you?"

Juliet cocked her head, her eyes flitting toward the window in the tent, where the woods were just barely visible outside. "It matters," she said slowly, "because I want in."

Wombat burst out laughing. "You want us to trust a Lifer?"

"That's like trying to catch a cloud," Rigby said. "Which I've tried. Believe me, it's not possible."

Smalls ignored them, studying Juliet. "You're serious."

Juliet lowered her voice. "I want out of this place. And I want Hamlet to come with me. Before one of us ends up like May—with no monkey sanctuary to save us."

Smalls met her eyes. He saw that word reflected back at him. *Freedom.* "Okay," he said suddenly. "You're in."

Wombat and Rigby's jaws dropped. "She's *what?*" they both asked.

"Think about it," Smalls said. "They're lions. We could use their strength. Besides, leaving in the middle of the show was really her idea."

Wombat lowered his voice. "How can we be adequately sure we can trust them, Smalls?"

Smalls looked back at Juliet. She seemed tired, he thought. Worn. As if she were carrying it all on her back—the threats, the slop, the fights, the punishments. "You can trust us," she promised. "We'll help."

Wombat stared at her for a long moment. "Humans *do* have an abysmal fear of lions," he said tentatively.

Juliet bared her sharp fangs to demonstrate, and Rigby leapt backward. "So do Komondor dogs," he yelped.

"See?" Juliet flicked her tail against the ground. "You need us."

Wombat looked at Rigby. Rigby looked at Wombat. Smalls could see a message passing silently between them.

"Okay," Wombat said.

"Okay," Rigby said.

"But no others can know about it in advance," Wombat added. "The last thing we need is Lord Jest or Buck thwarting our plans."

Juliet nodded. "Thank you," she said softly. For a second, Smalls thought he saw a glimmer of tears in her eyes. But then she blinked and it was gone. "Now let's get planning."

Chapter Forty-three

Better Than a Squirrel

Susan couldn't find Bertie anywhere. She'd looked in the Big Top, in his sleeping caravan, even in the kitchen, but it was like he'd just disappeared. And right when she was dying to tell him about her parents' letters. "Where *is* he?" she muttered. The only place she hadn't looked was the woods, but why would he be there?

"Of course," she blurted. Her cave. Why hadn't she thought of it before? She'd been the one who told him to go there. She took off running, clutching her parents' most recent letter in her hands. It was the one written only days ago. She'd hidden the rest of them safely under her bed, but she couldn't make herself part with this one. It was proof that they were real—not just the letters, but the parents too.

She was panting by the time she reached the cave, and she paused outside to catch her breath. All around her the woods were alive with whispers, wind skirting through the trees, making the leaves rattle and fall. There was a thickness to the air too, like you could scoop it right up in your hands. A storm was coming, Susan realized.

She only hoped it would pass before nighttime. A caravan was the worst place to weather out a storm. The rain pounded against the roof so loudly it seemed to be thrumming inside you, and the wind shook the caravan back and forth, back and forth, like a boat on a violent sea. Without fail, one of the Nillings always threw up, and with the windows sealed up tight, the stench would seep into everything, impossible to escape.

When her breathing returned to normal, Susan pushed her way into the cave. From the outside, the cave didn't look like much, just a solid wall of gray rock. But there was an opening at the bottom, and when you ducked through it, the wall opened into a cavernous, empty space. Just like she'd predicted, Bertie was in there, sitting on the floor with his back to her. For a second, she saw the walls of the cave through his eyes. Paint was everywhere, bright, swirling, vibrant, a tornado of colors. It was like standing inside a canvas.

"Do I have news for you," she announced, dropping down next to him. She waved her parents' letter at him.

"That box we found was filled with letters, Bertie. And they were all from my parents. They want me. They've always wanted me. Claude's been lying to me all along." She tossed the letter into the air. "But not anymore. Somehow I'm going to find them."

"Claude's been lying about something else too," Bertie said, staring blankly at the letter as it fluttered into her lap. Only then did Susan notice the tears rolling silently down his cheeks.

She grabbed his arm. "What's wrong?"

"My mom is dead," he said dully. "She has been for years."

Susan closed her eyes. While she'd been finding her parents, Bertie had been losing his. "I'm so sorry," she said. She opened her eyes to find him staring straight ahead, at the field of wildflowers she'd painted across the wall.

"I'm all alone," he said. "I have no one. No family."

Susan picked her letter back up, bending it between her fingers. She was thinking of something her mom had said to her once. "When I was little," she told Bertie, "I used to see this duck wandering around our farm, always waddling after the same family of squirrels. Finally one day I asked my mom if the duck was confused and thought he was a squirrel. 'Of course not,' my mom told me. 'He knows he's a duck. But sometimes you can find family in surprising places.'" Susan turned to Bertie. His bright blue eyes were clouded over with tears. "You just have to find your squirrels," she said softly.

Bertie stood up. Walking over to the wall, he ran his finger along the curve of a flower. Silence yawned through the cave, and he realized vaguely that he should say something, fill it. But he was too busy working through what Susan had just said. *Sometimes you can find family in surprising places.*

Out of nowhere, he pictured Smalls, his long tongue reaching out to lick his hand. He wasn't a squirrel, but he was even better. "I have to go," he said suddenly. All day long, his head had been so fuzzy. But just like that, it cleared. "There's something I have to do." He started toward the opening of the cave.

"Wait!" Susan pulled a worn square of paper out from the waistband of her skirt. It was folded down the middle. "Here," she said, handing it to him. "I thought you'd want to see this. I found it in Claude's caravan."

Bertie looked down at it curiously. "Thanks." He paused by the opening. "I'm happy for you, Susan," he said, and he was surprised to find he really meant it. At least while he was losing his parents, someone else was finding hers. He gave her a small smile. "You're right, you should go find them," he added. Then he hurried out of the cave.

He unfolded the paper from Susan as he headed into the woods. But when he saw what it was, his legs stopped moving. It was a photograph of a young Claude, with his arm slung around a baby elephant. A note was scrawled across the back. *Claude and his best friend, Lord Jest—or Lordy as he calls him.*

Best friend? Bertie sucked in a breath. He'd always assumed Claude had been the same his whole life: selfish, cruel, *Claude.* If he imagined him as a boy, it was as a bully, spitting fingernails into teachers' faces and kicking stray cats on the street. But in this photo, he looked almost like Bertie.

Was it possible that once, a long, long time ago, Claude had been just like him? Bertie tried to imagine Claude and Lord Jest as best friends. Maybe Claude had taught the elephant tricks and scratched him under his chin and snuck food into his cage. Maybe he'd rooted for him when there was no one else to. And maybe once, when it felt like nothing was ever going to be right again, when he'd felt lower than the soles on the bottom of his shoes, he'd raised his voice and he'd called him worthless.

Bertie's mouth turned to chalk. If Claude had been just like him once . . . that meant one day he could be just like Claude. Bertie thought about how his anger had swallowed him up earlier until he felt like someone else altogether.

"*No,*" he whispered. It didn't matter how angry he was or how much his heart felt like it was splitting down the middle. He couldn't let anything turn him into that person—into Claude.

Bertie broke into a run. There was definitely, *definitely* something he had to do.

Next to him, Juliet burst out laughing. "Good one," she said, and Wombat lifted his snout, looking pleased.

"Even better," Claude told the twins. He took another double swig of cocoa, then wiped a smudge of chocolate off his lips. "Ames Howard!" Lloyd and Loyd stared at him blankly. "Who's Ames Howard?" Loyd asked hesitantly.

Claude narrowed his eyes at the twins. "Ames Howard is only one-half of the great Howard Brothers." He paused expectantly, but Lloyd and Loyd just kept staring at him blankly. "As in the Howard Brothers Circus?" Claude tried again.

"Oh!" Loyd gasped.

"Wow!" Lloyd exclaimed.

In the back of the ring, the Misfits and Juliet all fell silent. Everyone in the world knew of the Howard Brothers Circus. It was the largest, grandest, most popular circus of all time.

"Ames Howard was at our show last night," Claude said. "Because the Howard Brothers were thinking about buying the Most Magnificent Traveling Circus."

"Oh," Loyd said hesitantly.

"Wow," Lloyd said tentatively.

"Buying?" Smalls whispered.

"Of course, after our disastrous finale," Claude contin-ued, "Ames went sprinting out of the tent. I was sure I'd never hear from him again! But then . . ." He paused to down more hot cocoa. "But *then*, just now while I was getting my cocoa, he called." Claude did a little jump in the air. "I was able to convince him that the fire was caused by faulty equipment, not faulty performers. And he *believed* me! They've decided they still want to buy the Most Magnificent Traveling Circus! They're going to send it overseas."

Loyd furrowed his brow. "You mean to the other side of a pond?" he asked.

"Of course not," Lloyd said impatiently. "He means to the other side of a creek. Right, Boss?"

Claude sighed. "Across the *ocean*, boys. To other countries, other continents!"

"Which countries?" Loyd asked.

"Which continents?" Lloyd added.

Claude shrugged. "Who knows? Who cares? All I know is that they're paying us! I can retire at last! And you, boys, will get nice, fat bonuses if you decide to stay with the circus."

Loyd and Lloyd threw their arms around each other, cheering with joy. Claude waved his top hat for silence. "There's just one thing. They want the circus to leave tomorrow. We'll have one last performance tonight, and then first thing tomorrow, we head to the harbor."

Smalls, who'd been listening carefully to the exchange,

took a sudden step back. Tomorrow? The circus was going overseas tomorrow?

Claude threw an arm around both of the Lloyds. "Come on, Lloyd. Come on, Loyd. We're taking an early lunch today to celebrate! I'm getting a steak on Mr. Ames Howard!" As Claude, Lloyd, and Loyd ambled out of the Big Top, Smalls looked anxiously from Wombat to Rigby to Juliet.

"Tomorrow," Juliet said uneasily.

"Which means if we're going to escape," Smalls said, "we're going to have to do it tonight."

Chapter Forty-five

Eat Fingernails

Seconds after Claude, Lloyd, and Loyd left, Bertie came flying into the Big Top. He was panting as he ran over to Smalls, beads of sweat clinging to his forehead. Rigby, Wombat, and Juliet had been huddled together with Smalls, whispering about escape plans, but they all backed away quickly, giving Smalls his space.

Bertie threw his arms around Smalls's neck, hugging him tightly. "I'm sorry," he whispered. "I'm so sorry. I'm sorrier than a firefly in a jar." He blinked. That saying had just popped right out of his mouth. But it felt familiar somehow. Where had he heard it before? "I'm sorrier than a firefly in a jar," he said again. He closed his eyes, and suddenly the memory that had been tugging at his mind since he found that wooden boy came floating into his reach.

He was outside. It was nighttime, but specks of light were

flashing in the darkness. He was holding a glass jar, chasing wildly after the specks as they flitted in and out of sight. "Got you!" he yelled, slamming the lid on his jar. Inside, a firefly skittered frantically, hitting up against the walls of the jar.

"Bertie!" His mom stuck her head outside, her red hair like a flame in the starlight. "Dinner's ready."

"I'm too busy to eat," Bertie declared. "I'm sorry, Mom."

His mom eyed the jar in his hand. The firefly was flickering brightly inside. "I bet you're not sorrier than that firefly in a jar," she said. She came outside, gently taking the jar out of his hands. Unscrewing the lid, she released the firefly. It flashed once, then disappeared into the night.

"Hey," Bertie protested. "It took me almost an hour to catch him!"

His mom pulled something out of the pocket of her apron, a miniature wooden boy with painted blue eyes and a shock of red hair escaping his tiny wooden baseball cap. She dropped it into the jar with a smile. "*This* you can trap in a jar," she said.

Bertie opened his eyes. The glass jar was gone, and so was his mom. Instead, Smalls stood in front of him, pressing his muzzle into Bertie's hand. Bertie scratched him under his chin, right where he knew he liked it, and said what he'd come to say. "You're my family now, Smalls."

Smalls leaned into Bertie's hand. "Family," he repeated.

He felt warm and gooey all over, as if he'd been dipped in honey. He stuck out his long tongue and gave Bertie's hand a lick. "I forgive you," he said.

Bertie touched the wooden doll in his pocket, comforted by the sound of Smalls's grunts. He wondered if Smalls was talking to him, in his own, bear way. *I forgive you,* he imagined him saying.

"If only we could get out of this place," Bertie said with a sigh. "If only we could run away somewhere together."

An idea struck Smalls. "Maybe we can," he whispered.

Plop-plop-plop! Several raindrops splashed down on the top of the tent, the noise echoing through the ring. Smalls looked toward the window. Outside, the sky had turned dark and gray, clouds gathering and colliding, cloaking the sun like a curtain. "Those are not friendly clouds," he heard Rigby pant. "Those are Claude clouds."

"Storm clouds," Juliet assessed.

Bertie scratched Smalls under his chin. "There's something I need to do," he whispered. "But don't forget what I said, okay? You're my family now, Smalls. I promise I'll never hurt you again."

As Bertie hurried out of the tent, a small square of paper slipped out of his pocket, fluttering to the ground. Smalls lumbered over to it, his chains digging into his paws. It was a photo, Smalls realized. He crouched down to get a better look. In the photo, a boy had his arm draped around a baby elephant.

"Aww." The sound of Lord Jest's sneer drew Smalls's attention away from the photo. "You and that boy are just soooo sweet," he said, clomping over to Smalls. He shook his head, making his ears flap through the air like wings. "When ya gonna listen to me, buddy bear? Caring only gets ya in . . ." Lord Jest trailed off as his eyes landed on the photo on the floor. "Where did that come from?" he asked sharply.

"It fell out of Bertie's pocket. It's a photo of—"

"I know what it's of," Lord Jest interrupted, his voice tense. "I just don't want to see it!" Lifting a chained hoof, he gave the photo a kick, sending it flying to the other side of the ring. "Why would Bertie even have it?"

Smalls watched Lord Jest smack his trunk angrily against the floor. Suddenly, a thought dawned on him. "The elephant in that picture . . . was that you, Lord Jest?"

"So what if it was?" Lord Jest spit out. "It was a lifetime ago. Back when Claude still had a heart," he added under his breath.

Smalls took a step back in surprise. The boy in that picture, *hugging* the elephant . . . "That was *Claude*?" he whispered.

Lord Jest let out a nasty honk. "It's like I was saying before, caring only gets ya in trouble."

Smalls blinked as he stared up at the elephant. He finally understood. Lord Jest wasn't mean because he was angry. Lord Jest was mean because he was *hurt*. Claude had been his friend once, and he'd betrayed him. Smalls thought about how terrible he'd felt after Bertie had yelled at him, like something inside him had shattered. How long had Lord Jest felt like that?

"It doesn't have to be that way," Smalls said softly. He pictured Bertie: his smile, his laugh, the way he'd said that word, *family*. Suddenly, he felt unbearably sad for Lord Jest. He stepped closer to the elephant, looking him right in the eyes. "Sometimes the trouble is worth it."

Outside the Big Top, Bertie was on his way to find his uncle. It wasn't Claude's usual lunchtime yet, so if he wasn't in the tent, there was only one other place he was likely to be: filling up on cocoa in his caravan. As Bertie made his way there, he replayed his new memory over and over again. It felt like such a gift, to remember. For so long his mind had been like the dusty ground here: dry and barren, a place where nothing could grow. But now something *had*. And maybe if one memory could sprout, more would too. He reached into his pocket, toying with the tiny wooden doll tucked inside. His mom had given him one just like it. But why? And when? He fought hard to remember—to make another memory sprout—but the answers eluded him.

He slowed down as he neared Claude's caravan. He could worry about the memory later. Right now, he had his uncle to face. "Uncle," he practiced. "You can't treat me like a little boy anymore. If I'm going to stay here, I demand you treat me better from now on. And I demand you treat the animals better too!" *Demand.* He liked that. He pushed his baseball cap off his forehead. From now on, he decided, there would be no more yeses.

Taking a deep breath, he flung open the door to the caravan. "Uncle?" he called out, stepping inside. But the caravan was dark and still. Claude wasn't there. Bertie closed the door behind him, looking around. He was rarely allowed in his uncle's caravan, and he couldn't help but stare at all the space he had, enough room for a whole couch and a table and a long counter. At the very end of the counter, his eyes landed on a tall ceramic urn.

Bertie pulled the top off it, peering inside. It was Claude's cocoa powder. Reaching into his pocket, he felt for the fingernail Claude had spit out at him last night. It was still right where he'd dropped it. "Eat fingernails, Uncle," he said, tossing the nail into the urn. As he did, he noticed a

piece of paper peeking out from beneath the cocoa powder. It was a check, written out to C. Magnificence. Bertie's jaw dropped as he stared at the number on the check. *For the rabbit,* someone had written along the bottom.

Bertie thought back to the animals that had been in the tent. He'd been so consumed by his anger earlier that he'd barely noticed anything. But as he ran through the animals in his head, it hit him that Tilda the Angora rabbit hadn't been there. *He sold her.* It dawned on him suddenly. Claude had sold the rabbit. He looked down at the check, gripping it tightly in his fingers.

"This shouldn't be yours," he whispered angrily. Without stopping to think, he stuck the check into his pocket. Then he placed the top back on the urn and hurried out of the caravan. Outside, the rain was picking up, and the sky had turned dark and threatening overhead. But he barely noticed. Because Claude's unattended urn of cocoa had given him an idea.

Bertie broke into a smile as he climbed into his caravan. Pushing past the clowns, he went into his closet of a bedroom, wrangling the jar of Claude's nails out from under his bed. "It's time you go where you belong," he said. "Into the cocoa." Clutching the jar to his chest, he started back to Claude's caravan.

Chapter Forty-six
Toddle's Toys

"Let's run through it one more time," Smalls said, his chains clanging against the ground as he paced nervously along the back of the ring. There were only two hours left until showtime, and as Lloyd and Loyd patched up any remaining damage from last night's fire, Smalls, Wombat, Rigby, Juliet, and Hamlet were putting the final touches on their escape plan.

"First," Juliet began, "the fangs will take care of the identical baboons."

"As well as the rooster," Hamlet added, licking his chops. "He won't rule the roost after this!"

"Good," Smalls said with a nod. They were using code words so Buck and Lord Jest wouldn't know what they were planning. When the time came, the elephant and zebra could escape with the rest of them, but until then, Smalls wasn't taking any chances.

"Next, the Hairy-Nosed Prince will get Blackie set up for our special grand finale," Wombat said proudly.

"And the Four-Legged Rainbow will delay the watchers!" Rigby chimed in.

"And then finally, the chickens will all fly the coop," Smalls finished.

"Chickens?" Buck muttered. "Rainbow? What are they *talking* about?" He looked over at Lord Jest, but Lord Jest ignored him, staring blankly into the distance.

"All right," Smalls said. He looked from Wombat to Rigby to the lions. "Here goes nothing."

A few hours later, Bertie stood at the back of the Big Top, watching Buck and the lions perform their tricks in the ring. Something felt different at the circus tonight, Bertie decided. He'd noticed it every time he'd taken a break from the concession stand to peek his head in to watch. There was an electric buzz to the air, as if somewhere in the tent, lightning had struck.

It could just be the weather, Bertie reasoned. It had grown steadily worse since this morning until a full-blown storm was raging, rain pounding and thunder clapping and wind howling, making the lights flicker out occasionally in the ring. Or maybe, Bertie thought, it was him. Between his new memory and the stunt he'd pulled with Claude's cocoa, Bertie had been feeling antsy all night. Something had to change; he knew that much. He just didn't know what it was.

The animals disappeared backstage, and Susan swung in on her rope. The tips of her long blond hair were wet from the rain, but the audience didn't seem to notice. They oohed and aahed in all the right places as she twirled her way through the ring. She caught Bertie's eye as she leaned into her back bend, giving him a tiny smile. Bertie smiled back. Whether it was the storm or it was him, something was definitely buzzing through the air, and it was making him want to *do* something.

"Hello!" a woman called out from the concession area, making Bertie jump. "Is there anyone to buy soda from around here?"

Bertie slipped through the curtain back to the soda counter. "What can I get you?" he asked. Just days ago, he would have been terrified that Claude would find out he'd abandoned his post, but right now it was the last thing on his mind. He looked up and found himself staring into the face of the same pale, watery-eyed woman he'd served last night. The one whose awful daughter had worn that poufy yellow dress.

"One cola," the pale-faced woman ordered primly. She

was with a friend, a large woman whose chin quivered and wobbled with every movement.

"What a disgrace this circus is!" the wobbly-chinned woman said in disgust. "Next time, I'm insisting my daughter wait until the Howard Brothers Circus is in town. I heard there was even a fire in the ring last night!"

The pale-faced woman nodded. "There was. I was here. And believe me, I did not want to return for a second viewing. But Chrysanthemum seemed to find the whole fire rather exciting. She insisted we return again tonight. And you know my Chrysanthemum. She's impossible to say no to." She let out a nervous laugh. "If I didn't know better, sometimes I'd think she was trying to punish me for something!"

Probably because you named her Chrysanthemum, Bertie thought.

"How is she liking that circus rabbit you got her?" the wobbly-chinned woman asked as Bertie handed the pale-faced woman her cola.

Bertie looked up sharply. *Circus rabbit?*

"Two colas for me," the wobbly-chinned woman commanded when she noticed Bertie staring at them. Bertie nodded, pouring the sodas as slowly as possible so he could catch more of their conversation.

"Chrysanthemum won't put that white puff ball down."

The pale-faced woman laughed. "She keeps calling it her purse and trying to hang it in her closet! That's my Chrysanthemum for you. Her parents own Toddle's Toy Emporium, and she manages to find the only toy out there that we don't sell!"

"Soon enough, she'll have you opening a pet store too." The wobbly-chinned woman tittered.

"Probably," the pale-faced woman agreed. "Filled with hundreds of Angora rabbits named Tilda."

At the sound of Tilda's name, Bertie lost his grip on one of the cups, sending it splattering to the floor.

"Careful, little boy!" the wobbly-chinned woman scolded. She jumped out of the way as a stream of cola shot out of the cup, making her chin wobble even faster.

Bertie murmured something: *sorry,* maybe, or *my apologies.* He couldn't be sure; he was too busy rehashing what the woman had just said. Tilda was at some place called Toddle's Toy Emporium.

"The boy must be slow," the wobbly-chinned woman said, snatching the other cup out of Bertie's hand.

The pale-faced woman tossed a coin at Bertie before hooking arms with her friend. "I bet they don't hire slow boys at the Howard Brothers Circus," Bertie heard her say as they stalked back to the ring.

"Didn't you hear, ladies?" A man with a long, curling mustache stopped them by the curtain. "The Howard Brothers Circus just bought this old rig. They're sending it overseas tomorrow."

"The Howard Brothers Circus is going to take over everything," the wobbly-chinned woman said knowingly before disappearing through the curtain.

"Overseas?" Bertie whispered. Abandoning the soda counter, he hurried back to the ring. His mind was suddenly tugging him in a million directions at once. Tilda was at Toddle's Toy Emporium. Claude had sold the circus. The Howard Brothers were sending them overseas. And then once again, unbidden, the memory from earlier: the way his mom had smiled as she'd pulled out the wooden boy. His fingers tightened around the wooden boy in his pocket. *Something has to change*, he thought again. *And quick.*

Chapter Forty-seven

Something's Fishy and It's Not Tuna

"L oyd, Lloyd, line the animals up," Claude ordered. "It's time for my final finale!"

"And ours too," Juliet murmured as Loyd yanked her into line.

"What was that, Juliet?" Buck asked suspiciously. When Juliet didn't answer, Buck flicked his tail impatiently. "I smell something fishy," he declared. "And it's not tuna. You and Hamlet have been whispering way too much with those Misfits today. Right, Lord Jest?"

But Lord Jest didn't reply. He was swishing his trunk back and forth through the air, his eyes distant.

"We were simply playing a word game," Wombat jumped in. "It's called . . . Word Filler." He named one of his favorites of Smalls's games. As Wombat jumped into a long-winded explanation of the rules of Word Filler, Rigby retreated behind his fur.

"You're a brave, graceful dog," he whispered, giving himself a pep talk. "You're a strong, capable dog."

Smalls looked over at Juliet. "The oil's in the bucket?" he asked.

"Hamlet took care of it," she said.

"And the paint's ready to go?" Smalls already knew the answer, but he felt the need to check just once more. Their whole escape was resting on this finale. If anything went wrong, they'd be sent overseas tomorrow, and any last hope of finding Tilda would vanish.

"Rigby knows where it is," Juliet said. "Don't worry, Smalls. We're ready."

Smalls nodded, but he couldn't help wishing for the millionth time that he had a four-leaf clover to calm his nerves.

"Places," Claude announced. "Go!"

Someone pushed Smalls on the rump, sending him stumbling into the ring. Above him, the lights flickered unsteadily as the wind beat against the flaps of the tent. In the audience, a boy started crying. "I'm scared, Mom," he said.

Sorry, kid, Smalls apologized silently. *But it's about to get a whole lot scarier.*

The circus horn blasted once, twice. It must have blasted another time too, but the sound was drowned out by a clap of thunder. Outside, lightning flashed, brightening the tent for a single instant. With a twirl of Lord Jest's trunk, the finale began.

Lord Jest crouched down, allowing Susan to climb onto his back. As he rose onto his stool, he began tossing hoops into the air. If Smalls had been watching Lord Jest, he might have noticed the way he stared straight ahead as he performed, his eyes glassy and unfocused. He might have noticed how his hoops, usually thrown with such finesse and precision, teetered a little as they slid down over Susan. And he might have heard the words he kept repeating to himself, over and over, like a mantra. "Sometimes the trouble is worth it."

But Smalls was too preoccupied with his own plans to pay any attention to Lord Jest. The finale continued on. Juliet and Hamlet began to spin on their wheel, Buck juggled balls alongside them, Wombat mounted his tightrope, and Rigby lay balanced on his beach ball, hiding beneath his fur.

As Smalls took his place behind his hoop of fire, a pesky list began to form in his mind. *Things That Could Go Wrong*. He closed his eyes, trying desperately to banish it. *Four-leaf clovers*, he thought. He pictured a field of them, hundreds upon hundreds, blossoming and unfolding before his eyes. A bubbling stream of honey wound through them, steam wafting off it.

When Smalls opened his eyes again, Juliet and Hamlet had almost reached Lord Jest. The elephant straightened out his trunk and Susan got ready to slide down it. But at the last minute, the lions steered away. They spun wildly toward the back of the ring, heading for backstage.

That was his cue. In a single bound, Smalls had reached Lord Jest.

"Whoa!" Susan cried out as she landed on Smalls's back instead of Juliet's.

Meanwhile, Hamlet and Juliet crashed through the curtain. The entire backstage fell still. The tumblers stopped stretching. The clowns stopped snickering. Loyd and Lloyd stopped cleaning. And Claude stopped shining his top hat.

"W-what the . . . ?" Loyd stuttered.

"H-how the . . . ?" Lloyd stammered.

"Why the . . . ?" Claude gasped.

The lions ignored them all. "You know, Juliet," Hamlet said, "I've always thought the wrong siblings were trapped in a cage."

"I think it's about time we remedied that, Hamlet," Juliet agreed. The lions rolled their wheel straight toward the twins. "Now!" Juliet called out, and in unison they leapt off, sending the wheel crashing down—trapping Loyd and Lloyd underneath it.

"Hey!" Loyd flailed around, kicking his brother. "I can't move!"

"No, *I* can't move!" Lloyd thrashed around, hitting his brother.

"The beautiful sound of brotherly love." Hamlet sighed.

Juliet laughed. "Now it's *his* turn." The lions spun around to face Claude, who was backing up into the wall of the tent.

"Lloyd," Claude hissed. "Loyd! Get off your lazy butts and stop these lions!"

But Lloyd and Loyd just thrashed helplessly under the wheel.

Hamlet bared his razor-sharp fangs. "This," he said, "is going to be fun."

Chapter Forty-eight

The Moment of Truth

Susan looked around, flabbergasted, as Smalls deposited her in the center of the ring. To her left, Rigby leapt to his feet on the beach ball, tossing the fire sticks over to Wombat. Wombat caught them in his teeth, and Rigby jumped to the ground, disappearing backstage. Susan tugged on a strand of hair. Something was going on. It was almost as if the animals had some sort of plan.

She felt something soft press against her ankle, and she looked down to see Wombat nudging her with his snout. With a grunt, he tossed the fire sticks up to her. She caught them automatically and Wombat nudged her again, nodding his snout toward Smalls.

He wanted her to throw the fire sticks, she realized. She glanced over at the audience, who were all watching expectantly, oblivious to the fact that the finale had suddenly, somehow gone haywire. From backstage, she heard some-thing that sounded vaguely like a scream.

Yes, she thought. *Something is definitely going on.*

Excitement rose inside her. Ever since she'd read those letters from her parents, she'd felt like she couldn't sit still. All day long, her mind had whirred and clacked and churned, a machine spinning its wheels. Something had to change, she knew. The question was: *how?*

Wombat gave her another nudge. His eyes were wide and round. Whatever the animals were planning, she was going to help. Quickly, she lit the fire sticks, raising the first one into the air. As she threw it, Smalls tucked his legs, leaping easily through the hoop of fire.

"This is for you, Bertie," Smalls whispered, landing softly on all fours. Stretching out his tongue, he caught the first fire stick flawlessly. Behind him, the audience cheered, and for a second Smalls felt a flicker of that old thrill he used to get at Mumford's when he knew the crowd had arrived. He caught the second fire stick and then the third and the fourth, keeping his eyes trained on the curtain at the back of the ring. Everything depended on what hap-pened next.

As Smalls snatched the last fire stick out of the air, Juliet and Hamlet burst out through the curtain, dragging Claude into the ring by his coattails. "Let me go!" Claude was screaming. "Free me this instant!"

"Sorry," Juliet said. "But it's about time *we* get to be free." As she and Hamlet leapt out of the way, Smalls flicked his tongue, winging each of the fire sticks at Claude. They landed in a tight circle, surrounding him in flames.

"Let's see *you* jump through a ring of fire," Smalls told Claude.

Inside the circle of flames, Claude's face turned beet red as a line of sweat sprang to his brow. "Water!" he screeched, his nasal whine ringing through the tent. "Spray water, Lord Jest!"

But Lord Jest didn't move a muscle.

"Water!" Claude thundered. "Now!"

Still Lord Jest didn't move. "Sometimes the trouble is worth it," he whispered.

"Now, Lord Jest, or you're going to have a nice, long run-in with Wilson tonight!" Claude went on.

Lord Jest let out a whimper. "And sometimes it isn't." He dunked his trunk in the bucket of water.

"Here we go," Wombat murmured. "The moment of truth."

Lord Jest lifted his trunk, taking aim. But what sprayed out wasn't water. It was oil.

Wombat burrowed his paws excitedly. "Just as I predicted. When you mix oil and water, the oil always rises to the top."

Lord Jest blinked. "Ya tricked me."

The oil landed in a perfect arc around Claude. But instead of putting out the fire like water would have, it intensified it. As flames shot up to the ceiling, Claude howled with fury. "He sounds like a hyena," Buck grumbled, and for once Smalls had to agree with the zebra.

In the audience, people were leaping to their feet. "Not *again*," one woman cried.

"Now, Rigby!" Smalls called out. It was time to paint this ring red.

Rigby tore through the curtain, a bucket gripped in his teeth. Hurrying to the front of the ring, he nosed the bucket onto its side. Red paint spilled out, coating the floor along the edge of the seats. Several splotches got on Rigby too, and his eyes widened as he looked down at the red streaks on his fur. "I'm ruby-colored," he breathed.

Behind him, Claude let out another howl. "Someone stop those wild animals!" he shouted.

"I'll get 'em," a burly man with a thick black beard offered.

He jumped down from his seat, grabbing for Rigby. But as he did, his foot landed in a patch of red paint, slipping

out from beneath him. "Holy mackerel!" he shouted as he flew through the air, landing with a thud on his butt.

"I think you mean holy horseshoe," Smalls said happily.

As others leapt out of their seats, trying to grab for the animals or make for the exit, they too hit slippery, gooey patches of paint. Legs went slipping out from beneath people left and right. Skirts flapped up and coats flew open and butts hit the floor, one after another.

"My brand-new skirt!" a pale-faced woman screeched as she slid across the floor, colliding headfirst with the bearded man.

"Fireeeee!" a wobbly-chinned woman cried out as she slipped along the floor, slamming butt-first into a furious-looking grandfather.

"The Four-Legged Rainbow has delayed the audience!" Rigby called out to the others.

"Stop those animals!" Claude continued yelling, ignoring Rigby's barks. "They're wild! They need to be in cages!"

Smalls let out a deep roar, which the animals knew meant one thing and one thing only. *Run.*

Immediately, Wombat and Rigby headed for the tent's exit, with Hamlet close behind them. "Come on, Lifers," Hamlet shouted. "We're breaking free!"

"I *knew* something fishy was going on," Buck growled.

Kicking up his hooves, he took off after the animals. "Let's go, Lord Jest," he shouted over his shoulder.

But Lord Jest just stood there, his eyes wide with fear.

"Come on, Lord Jest!" Buck tried again. But when Lord Jest still didn't move, he left without him.

Outside, rain drenched the animals instantly, washing the paint off Rigby and matting their fur down flat. Rigby shook drops of water out of his eyes as he raced toward the woods, his gait sure and steady in spite of the mud. Hamlet was a few feet ahead of him, his long legs eating up the ground.

Behind them, Wombat wasn't faring nearly as well. The short, stout paws that were perfect for burrowing a hole in three seconds flat were good for nothing in the mud. "Rigby!" he called out as he sank rapidly into the ground. "I need assistance!" But his words were snatched away by the wind. "Rigby!" He tried again. But it was useless. Rigby kept running, oblivious to Wombat's cries.

Buck, who had paused to look back once more for Lord Jest, found himself staring at a flailing hairy-nosed wombat. Wombat was yanking at his paws, trying desperately to fight through the mud, but it wasn't getting him anywhere. Buck let out an annoyed sigh. "Fine," he grumbled, marching back to Wombat. He stopped next to him, crouching down low. "Hop on."

Wombat's jaw dropped open. "You'd like me to . . . ?" He trailed off, at a rare loss for words.

"Do you want to escape or not?" Buck snapped.

Wombat leapt onto Buck's back, clutching his mane with his paws. "Let's vamoose," he declared. "Let's skedaddle. Let's hightail it. Let's—"

"Let's shut up if you want a ride," Buck interrupted.

Wombat snapped his mouth shut. "My snout is sealed."

Buck nodded. "Now let's—how did you say it?—*vamoose*." He took off sprinting through the rain with Wombat on his back.

Meanwhile, in the doorway of the tent, Juliet paused. "What are you waiting for, Smalls?" she called back. "It's time to go!"

Smalls scanned the tent. His eyes fell on Bertie, who was leaping over Rigby's river of paint to get to Susan. "You go ahead," Smalls told Juliet. "There's something I have to do first." He galloped over to Bertie. "You said you wanted to run away together," he said. Then he grabbed Bertie's suspenders in his teeth.

Chapter Forty-nine

Worth the Trouble

Smalls had Bertie's suspenders in his teeth, and he was tugging him toward the exit. Something kicked alive in Bertie's chest. The animals were escaping. He'd known it, in some form, since the second he saw Smalls throw those fire sticks at Claude.

"Bertie!" Claude yelled from inside the ring of fire. "Get me out of here right now! Or I'll, I'll . . ."

He said something else, but Bertie didn't hear. The wind had blown the door to the tent wide open, and suddenly Bertie could see outside. Rain slashed down in sheets and the wind tossed mud and dust through the air, but it was something else that caught his eye. In the sky, through a crack in the clouds, he saw a single star, burning through the grayness and the darkness and the storm.

He blinked, once, twice, three times, but the star remained, shining steadily away. It made Bertie think of time, how even in the worst of storms, the earth kept right on spinning. *There are a million different paths out there,* he thought. *A million different directions. A million different possibilities.* Distantly, he felt Smalls tug on his suspenders. He heard Claude scream out his name. *It's about time I had an adventure,* he decided.

He looked over at Susan. "How about we go find your parents?" he said.

Susan broke into a grin. "You read my mind." She grabbed his hand. "Let's get out of here."

Smalls tugged Bertie's suspenders again, and this time Bertie went with him, Susan's hand clasped tightly in his.

Smalls let out a grunt of delight as he galloped out of the tent with Susan and Bertie at his side. Rain was pelting down on him, but he didn't care. He was running, legs cycling and muscles clenching and heart pounding, and there wasn't a chain or a cage or a wall in sight.

Up ahead, Juliet glanced over her shoulder. "You didn't," she said when she saw Susan and Bertie.

Smalls ducked in front of Susan to keep her from slipping in a pile of mud. "I did," he said. "Sometimes, I've learned, a little trouble is worth it."

Juliet sighed. "Well, holy horseshoe." She circled back and stopped in front of Susan, nudging her with her nose.

"Go ahead," she said. "Get on." Susan grabbed gratefully onto Juliet's neck. With the ease of an acrobat, she kicked herself onto the lion's back. "See you in the woods, Smalls," Juliet called out, taking off after the others.

Susan twisted around, looking back at Bertie. "Meet me in the cave!" she yelled, right before the wind swallowed up her voice.

Smalls knelt down next to Bertie. "Your turn," he said, lowering his neck for Bertie to grab on.

But Bertie wasn't an acrobat. He flung his arms around Smalls's neck, but every time he tried to kick himself up like Susan had, his feet went slipping and sliding in the mud, refusing to obey him.

"Come on, Bertie," Smalls pleaded. He looked nervously over his shoulder. People were spilling out of the tent in clumps, shielding themselves from the rain with umbrellas and newspapers and stolen food trays. "There's the bear!" someone yelled. "And a boy!"

Thunder clapped angrily in the sky, making the ground tremble beneath Smalls's paws. Bertie tried once more to throw himself on Smalls's back, but this time his hands slipped too, and he went plummeting to the ground.

"Coming through! Don't move! Let me by!"

Smalls tensed. That awful, nasal whine could only belong

to one person. He dove to the ground to help Bertie. As he did, something caught his eye. Something tiny and green, sprouting up from the wet, barren earth. Smalls's breath caught in his throat. A four-leaf clover. He grabbed the clover in his teeth as he nudged Bertie back up. *We could use some luck right now*, he thought.

"That bear is mine!" Over by the tent, Claude was fighting his way angrily through the crowd. Breaking into a sprint, he raced over to his motorcar, which was parked behind the Big Top. "You don't run from my circus and get away with it!" he shouted as he flung himself inside. Without bothering to shut the door, he gunned the engine, steering the motorcar toward Smalls and Bertie.

"But the rain," someone yelled as Bertie finally managed to swing his legs over Smalls, landing squarely on his back. "And the mud! If the car slides, you could hit them!"

Claude just kept on driving. "Then I hit them," he said.

"No!" Out of the tent burst Lord Jest, his ears flapping wildly as he raced toward Claude's motorcar. "Sometimes the trouble *is* worth it," he yelled.

Inside the car, Claude's eyes widened as he realized what the elephant was doing. "Stop," he screamed. But this time, Lord Jest didn't listen. Lifting his trunk, he dove right in front of the car.

Chapter Fifty

The Last Act

*K*A-BAM!

The sound rang out through the air as three thousand pounds of motorcar collided with thirteen thousand pounds of elephant. "Lord Jest!" Bertie screamed. He tightened his arms around Smalls's neck, nudging him toward the fallen elephant. "Come, on, Smalls, we have to help him!" But Smalls stayed frozen in place, his eyes flickering between the woods and Lord Jest.

Sirens blared in the distance as Claude leapt out of his motorcar. There was a deep scratch across his arm and he was limping, but it barely slowed him as he rushed to Lord Jest's side. He dropped down next to the elephant, a strange expression on his face. "Lordy," he whispered, placing a hand on the elephant's head. "Call a vet!" he cried out, and from somewhere in the distance came the faint sound of identical twins, responding in unison.

"We're on it, Boss!"

"Lordy," Claude said again, cradling the elephant's trunk. He looked up, and Smalls saw several tears rolling down his cheek.

"*Holy horseshoe,*" Smalls murmured. The strange expression on Claude's face was sorrow.

Bertie nudged Smalls again. "We have to go see if Lord Jest is okay!"

Smalls grunted. Bertie was right. He took off, galloping back toward the tent with Bertie clinging to his neck. But he'd only made it a few feet when he suddenly stopped short. Because rising above the rain and the thunder and the sirens was a familiar noise. The honk of an elephant—telling him to run for his life. "Turn around!" Lord Jest honked, his voice weak and raspy. "Save Bertie!"

Suddenly, Smalls understood. Lord Jest had done this for them. For *Bertie.* And the only way to truly thank him was to turn and to run.

Bertie clung desperately to Smalls's back as he veered sharply in the mud, steering them in the direction of the woods. He had no doubt why Smalls had turned around. He'd heard it too: Lord Jest's wild honk, directed right at them—as if he was telling them to run. Behind them, Bertie heard people yelling and rain slashing and sirens pulling up to the circus, one after another. He thought about twisting around, looking back. But he found himself looking forward instead, at the thick line of trees zooming toward them. At what lay ahead.

"Thank you, Lord Jest," he whispered.

The air smelled different as they neared the woods, sweeter and fresher, like someone had taken an eraser and wiped the world clean. Smalls let out an excited grunt when they crossed through the trees. Instantly, the world stilled. The sky became darker, the rain became thinner, even the sounds became quieter: trees creaking and leaves rustling and in the distance, the soft hoot of an owl.

Bertie slid off Smalls's back, his feet sinking into the muddy ground. "I think they're this way," he said, leading Smalls toward Susan's cave. As they walked, Bertie closed his eyes, tilting his head up toward the rain.

He was finally free: no one to yell at him, no one to punish him, no one to call him worthless. He had no idea what would happen next, but it didn't matter, because he'd be with his family. It was dark in the woods, but he felt like someone had flipped a switch inside his chest, lighting him up.

The rain eased to a thin drizzle as the cave came into view. Bertie broke into a smile when he saw the six wet, excited

faces waiting outside for him. "Took you long enough," Susan said with a grin. Walking over to Bertie, she threw her arms around him in a tight hug. "I'm glad you made it," she whispered.

Bertie watched as the animals ducked into the cave. Smalls went last, looking over his shoulder as if to say, "Come on!" Bertie grabbed Susan's hand. "Me too," he said.

Inside the cave, Smalls let out a deep, excited roar, like he used to at Mumford's when it was time to play a game. With his new four-leaf clover tucked behind his ear, he walked in a circle past each of his friends—his family—the new and the old. "So," he said. "What's next?"

Acknowledgments

This book wouldn't have been possible without the support and encouragement of so many people. HUGE thank you's to . . .

The Razorbill team, particularly Ben Schrank and of course Anne Heltzel—who's been an incredible editor and equally great friend.

Josh Adams and Adams Literary, for believing in my writing, and in me.

Randee Mendelsohn Segal, a teacher I'll never forget.

Eric and Monica Allon, who brought me to places like Cape Cod and Gloucester, where dreams always seemed within reach. And my "Brady Bunch" cousins, who were there to dream with me.

Popi, whose support and enthusiasm have always meant so much to me.

The whole Resnick/Wachtel family, who welcomed me in like one of their own.

Meryl Lozano, my reading-companion-almost-twin-partner-in-crime.

Lauren Nicole Greenberg, the most big-hearted person I know. Thank you for being my best friend, my backbone, and my biggest supporter, always.

The real Susan and Fred, neither acrobat nor wombat, but better parents than I could have dreamed up myself. Mom and Dad: you've allowed me to climb the highest trees and go out on every limb, because I knew you'd always be there to catch me if I fell. For that, I can't thank you enough.

And of course, my husband, Nathan, who knew just how long the path could be and still walked beside me every step of the way. I would have given up a thousand times already if it weren't for you (and probably eaten a thousand microwave dinners). You are in every word I write.

Finally, I want to thank my own four-legged companions, past and present: Maple, who during countless hours of writing never lets me get lonely. And Willow, who was the first to teach me that you don't need to speak the same language to be a true friend.

Keep reading for
a sneak peek at the sequel to

The Daring Escape of The Misfit Menagerie

in stores Fall 2013

In one fluid motion, Bertie yanked the wooden doll out of his pocket and handed it to Susan. "I found it on the circus grounds before we left." He said it so fast that the words came out in a big jumble, one bumping into another. Susan gave him a strange look as she lifted the wooden boy up to the sunlight, examining it. "It's not a doll," Bertie added hastily. "It's a wooden figurine, which is really very different because—"

"He looks like you," Susan interjected. She didn't seem the least bit concerned about whether it was technically a doll or a figurine. She touched a finger to the boy's bright red hair. "A lot like you, actually."

"That's why I took him," Bertie admitted. "That and . . . he reminds me of my mom." He blinked in surprise. He'd said it. And hearing it out loud, in his own voice, had actually felt *good*. "I have this memory of her giving the same kind of figurine to me when I was younger. When I look at him, it's like the fog in my head clears a little, and I can remember things about her again. Just bits and pieces: her voice, her hair, the way she laughs. But it's more than I've had in a long time."

"Like a memory trigger," Susan said thoughtfully. "We did an experiment like that in school once. All different things can trigger memories: smells, sounds, images."

"Well, what's *not* triggering a memory is this." Bertie reached over, turning the boy upside down so Susan could see the two green *T*'s stamped onto its foot. "I've been try-ing like crazy to figure out what it means."

Susan burst out laughing. "Every kid in America knows what that means!" She paused, her face darkening. "Well, every kid who didn't grow up with Claude *un*-Magnificence," she amended, crossing her eyes at the memory of Bertie's cocoa-swilling uncle. "It's the logo for Toddle's Toys."

Bertie plucked a blade of grass, wrapping it slowly around his finger. "Toddle's Toys," he repeated.

"Toddle's Toy Emporium is the biggest toy store in the country," Susan told him. "Probably even the world. I've never been, but kids at school used to talk about it all the time. It's this huge building supposedly, and it's filled with every toy imaginable, tons you've never even heard of before. . . ."

Susan might have continued, but Bertie had stopped

listening. Because in his head several pieces were suddenly clicking into place, one after another.

Toddle's Toy Emporium. An image of a watery-eyed woman flashed through his mind. That's where she'd said she'd taken Tilda! But he'd seen that name elsewhere, too.

Everything had happened so quickly the night of their escape that he'd forgotten all about the check he'd taken out of Claude's cocoa urn, the one inscribed with the words *For the rabbit.* Bertie dug into his pocket. *Please still be there*, he begged silently.

At the very bottom, he felt it: a thin sheet of paper coated in lint and crumpled into a ball. His breath released in fast spurts as he smoothed it out on the grass. *For the rabbit,* someone had written along the bottom, just like he remembered. Typed in the top left corner of the check was a name: *The Toddle Family.* And beneath that name was an address: *1 Toddle Lane, Hoolyloo City.*

Click. The final piece of the puzzle fell into place.

Tilda was at Toddle's Toy Emporium, the very place where Bertie's wooden boy had come from.

And he had the address.

He turned to Susan, a smile spreading across his face. "Looks like we're going to the biggest toy store in the world," he said.